NEVER LIE TO ME

ALSO BY A.M. STRONG & SONYA SARGENT

THE PATTERSON BLAKE THRILLER SERIES

Sister Where Are You

Is She Really Gone

All the Dead Girls

PATTERSON BLAKE PREQUEL

Never Lie to Me

NEVER LIE TO ME
A PATTERSON BLAKE PREQUEL

A.M. STRONG
SONYA SARGENT

WEST STREET

West Street Publishing

This is a work of fiction. Characters, names, places, and events are products of the author's imagination. Any similarity to events or places, or real persons, living or dead, is purely coincidental.

Copyright © 2021 by A. M. Strong & Sonya Sargent
All rights reserved.

No part of this book may be reproduced in any form or by any electronic or mechanical means, including information storage and retrieval systems, without written permission from the author, except for the use of brief quotations in a book review.

Cover art and interior design by Bad Dog Media, LLC.

ISBN: 9781942207221

10 9 8 7 6 5 4 3 2 1

For Gidget and Tiki, who I still think about!

ONE

THEY STOOD APART on the empty stage, two actors reciting their lines: Kaylee Roberts and Ben Ford, both in their early twenties. Before them, pacing like a caged tiger with a scowl on his face, was thirty-nine-year-old Jeremy Knight. Writer, director, and lead actor in the never-before-seen play, Midnight's Crossing.

Further away in the wings stood a huddle of other actors. Three males and two females. They all held scripts, their expressions betraying the exhaustion of a four-hour rehearsal that had stretched beyond seven. They had arrived at the theater before midday, excited for opening night less than a week away. But now, their enthusiasm had dissipated, replaced by weariness and hunger.

"Do you know what your problem is?" Knight asked, striding across the stage in anger. He fixed his female lead with a withering stare. "There's no fire in your gut. No passion. Do you know how important this is to me?"

"I'm doing my best, Jeremy." Kaylee's voice went up an octave in response to Knight's anger. She tugged at the hem of her blue skirt, a strand of blonde hair falling in front of her eyes. She held a dog-eared script with several pages marked by colored tabs. "I'm trying. I am. But you've made so many changes to the play over the last week. And we're so close to opening night. I think we should do the original lines. They were—"

"Nowhere near good enough," Knight interrupted. He threw his hands into the air before stalking away toward center stage, his hawkish face half illuminated by a lone floor light. He turned and faced the young actor. "No. The new lines are better. They're more dramatic. They capture the essence of these two characters. Speak to who they are."

"But—"

"The changes stay," Knight said, his voice strained. He closed his eyes briefly and took several deep breaths to steady himself. His expression softened. "Look, Kaylee, you're an excellent performer. A wonderful talent with a great career ahead of you. You can do this. I believe in you."

Kaylee nodded mutely. She lifted her script and thumbed through it, stopping at one of the tabbed pages. "You want us to do scene four again? I'll nail it this time. I promise."

"No." Jeremy had reached the end of his endurance. He glanced at his watch, moved downstage, then turned to face the group. "We're done. Rehearsal's over. All of you get out of here and find something to eat. It's been a long day. When you get home tonight, take some time to go over the new lines. Commit them to memory. We'll pick this up at rehearsal tomorrow when everyone's bright and fresh."

A murmur of appreciation rippled through the cast.

"Thank God for that," Ben said, his shoulders slumping with relief. The lighting crew and stagehands had been dismissed an hour ago rather than go into overtime. "I could do with a cold one."

"McGee's has happy hour 'till eight," said Eric Lane, one of the actors standing in the wings. He was referring to McGee's Irish Bar and Restaurant, a popular Main Street hangout in the swanky Long Island tourist town of Montauk. The eatery occupied a historic mock Tudor building a few blocks from the Phoenix Playhouse and was a favorite of the local performing community. "We can still make it."

"Works for me," Ben replied. He glanced at Kaylee. "How about you?"

"Sure." She closed her script and watched Ben head toward the wings, then turned back toward Jeremy, who hadn't moved. "You coming?"

"Soon." Jeremy gave her a wan smile. "I want to work on the revisions and check my blocking. Go ahead. I'll join you later."

"If you're sure," Kaylee said.

"Get out of here. I won't be long."

"Maybe I should stay and keep you company." She stepped toward him, reached out, and touched his arm.

"I'll be fine." He gave her a reassuring pat on the shoulder, then pulled his arm away.

"Kaylee, what are you doing? We're missing the cheap beer." Ben shouted from the wings. The rest of the cast had filed backstage already. He lingered in the doorway, waiting for her.

"You sure you don't want some company?"

"Yes." Jeremy nodded. He met her gaze. "I'm sure."

Kaylee bit her lip, nodded an acknowledgment, then started across the stage toward the wings. Then she turned and ran back, planting a quick kiss on his cheek. "Don't make me wait forever, okay?"

"I won't," he replied, knowing he wouldn't be joining her in the bar anytime soon and certainly not in time for happy hour. She knew it, too, even if she pretended not to. It was never less than an hour when he stayed behind, which he always did these days. There was so much to do, so many things to get right. "Scoot. I'll catch up with you at McGee's."

"Okay… Love you." Kaylee crossed the boards again, turned, blew him one more kiss, and then disappeared through the stage door.

He watched her go, then gazed across the rows of seats in the darkened auditorium. He felt a tingle of apprehension, just like he always did when alone in the theater. There was something about the place, a brooding melancholy that only dissipated when an audience was present. He thought all theaters felt that way when they were empty. Perhaps that was why there were so many ghost stories attached to them. Even the Phoenix had a phantom. The spirit of an ill-fated performer who couldn't bear to be parted from the stage he loved even in death. A spirit whose fleeting appearance doomed any show unlucky enough to be visited by him. At least if you believed the tall tales whispered by superstitious actors in the dressing rooms before curtain-up.

Knight shook off the strange feeling of disquiet and turned his attention back to the work at hand. He made his way toward the proscenium and the spot where he'd been standing before his cast left. He stared out into the darkness, replaying the last scene Kaylee and Ben had performed in his mind's eye. The problem was his female lead, he realized. Her delivery was forced. Her inflections were all wrong, and she over-articulated. He hated to admit it because he liked Kaylee, and she was beyond cute, but she wasn't a natural. He was in a real bind. There was no way he could replace her. Not now. The show was opening in a few days. Besides, he was invested in other ways. She had to stay, if only for an easy life.

He sighed and let his mind wander, hoping for a solution —some glimmer of inspiration that would put an end to his dilemma. But the answer was elusive. He was still reflecting on it fifteen minutes later when a jangling show-tune erupted from his pocket and broke his concentration.

Jeremy pulled out his cell phone and looked down at the screen, recognizing the number. He answered, then lifted the phone to his ear.

"Hey. I'm not done at the theater. I thought you were going to call later."

A moment's silence while he listened to the answer.

"No. It's fine. I'm happy to hear your voice."

Another beat.

"How do you think it's going? We've barely sold a ticket."

Jeremy listened. A smile touched his lips.

"Yeah. I miss you too. I can't wait to blow this place and get over there."

Beat.

"No, I haven't told anyone yet."

A faint noise from somewhere in the wings stage left. Maybe footsteps. Jeremy turned, wondering if one of the cast had returned. He hoped it wasn't Kaylee.

"Someone's here. I have to go. I'll call you tomorrow, okay?"

Beat.

"I can't wait to see you, either. A few weeks, and we'll finally be together." This last reply he whispered, then hung up quickly and returned the phone to his pocket.

Jeremy stared off into the dimly lit gloom at the side of the stage where he'd heard the noise. He could make out the props table, rolling scenery, and the cage that housed ropes and counterweights used to operate the fly system that raised and lowered scenery from the high roof above. But he didn't see Kaylee or anyone else.

He held his breath, listening. But all was silent now. Even so, the recently banished apprehension edged back, sending a shiver down his spine.

Get a grip. Nothing to be afraid of, he thought to himself.

But the inner voice did little to ease his nerves.

Jeremy decided enough was enough. He could pick it up tomorrow. He scooped his script from a stool at the front of the stage where he'd spent half the afternoon and evening perched as the rest of the cast ran their lines, jumping in and reciting his own lines by memory when necessary.

He turned toward the wings, intending to kill the lights,

lock the stage door, and get out of there. Retreat to the warm safety of McGee's and a double whiskey. Neat, of course.

But then another sound broke the silence. Like a door being eased open on old hinges.

He froze. It came from his rear, the direction of the orchestra pit. He swiveled, eyes searching the darkness beyond the footlights. "Hello?"

The quiet theater closed in around him. The air turned thick and heavy. The rows of seats beyond the apron looked like ghostly vessels waiting to be filled. He half expected to see a spectral figure occupying one of them, staring back at him, and was relieved when he didn't.

He fought back a glimmer of unreasoning panic, walked to the edge of the stage, and looked down into the gloomy orchestra pit that extended out from underneath the apron. He could have sworn the sound came from there. Had one of the actors snuck back in to give him a scare? He wouldn't put it past them.

"Anybody there?" he called out. "Ben, if that's you, I'm cutting all your lines and giving them to Eric."

No reply.

Only his own ragged breath and racing heartbeat filled his ears. If it *was* Ben, the goofy actor was taking things too far. But his churning gut told him it wasn't. He felt an overwhelming urge to get out. Something wasn't right. The atmosphere inside the old building was suffocating. As though he were standing inside a tomb.

Screw this, he thought, turning quickly upstage away from the pit.

Not quick enough.

Before he'd even taken a single step, a pair of hands grabbed at his ankles and yanked him backward with enough force that he lost his balance. He teetered on the edge of the stage before his feet slid off into empty air. He pitched forward, his body slamming into the front of the stage. He felt himself sliding down into the orchestra pit's yawning black maw. He reached out desperately to stop himself but felt only air between his fingers before he dropped into darkness. A moment later, his head struck something hard with an impact that left him stunned.

The pit's concrete floor.

The breath raced from his lungs. His shoulder was on fire, and he couldn't move his left arm. It must have broken when he hit the floor. But he didn't feel any real pain yet, which surprised him. Just a dull ache that spread out from the point of impact like ripples on a pond. He tried to get up, but his limbs refused to obey. He wanted to cry out, even as his throat constricted in panic. All he managed was a faint rattle.

Then he saw the figure, standing at the edge of his vision, swimming in and out of focus. A figure with a demonic face contorted in rage. And in its hand… a hammer.

TWO

MCGEE'S WAS SLOW, even for a Tuesday night. Kaylee returned from the bar with a pair of drinks, one clutched in each hand. She gave a pint to Ben, and kept the other for herself, then looked around. A pool table stood near the back of the room, three balls and a cue sitting atop it, the remains of the last game played. A darts board hung on the wall. Four guys sat around a table to her left. They were already there when she entered the bar and had been drinking for some time, judging by their loud conversation and raucous laughter. Apart from Kaylee's small group of actors, and a couple of folk lingering at the bar, drinks in hand, they were the only patrons.

She glanced at her watch. It had been almost an hour since she left Jeremy at the theater. That was long enough. She placed her drink on the table and turned to Ben. "Jeremy should be here by now. Let's go back to the theater and get him."

"Why?" Ben raised an eyebrow. "You know what Jeremy's like. He's probably rewriting the damn script again. He'll show up when he's good and ready. He always does."

"Please?" Kaylee leaned forward and did her best to look pitiful. "Pretty please?"

"All right. I'll come back with you." Ben gulped his beer and wiped suds from his mouth with the back of his hand. "Happy hour is over anyway."

"Thank you." Kaylee took a quick swig of her own drink, then stood up and started toward the door.

The rest of the group exchanged glances. They all knew what Kaylee was like with Jeremy.

Ben sighed and turned to leave. Kaylee was already halfway out of the door. He hurried to catch up. "Hey, wait for me."

It only took them a minute to walk the two blocks to the Phoenix. Kaylee was striding along like a woman on a mission. When they reached the theater, she turned left into a narrow alley running between the Phoenix and a scented candle store that occupied the building next door.

They entered through the unlocked stage door and made their way past the green room and a concrete staircase leading down to the dressing rooms under the stage. The offices were down there, too, along with orchestra pit access. The stairwell was illuminated by a single wall-mounted light fixture. As they passed by, Kaylee glanced down into the gloom before continuing on to a door leading into the wings. The same door they had left through an hour before.

She pulled it open and hurried onto the stage, but there was no sign of Jeremy.

She made her way to the middle and stood there, hands on hips. "Where is he?"

"Beats me," Ben said. "Maybe he went down to the dressing rooms."

"Maybe." Kaylee glanced around.

"Or he could have finished up and gone home."

"I doubt it," Kaylee said. "He wouldn't do that without letting me know. Besides, the footlights are still on, and the stage door is unlocked."

"Just call him." Ben paced to the rear of the stage and peeked behind the white canvas drop that hid the back wall and large loading bay doors where the scenery was brought in. He turned and walked back toward Kaylee as she took her phone out.

She unlocked the screen and found Jeremy's name on her call log. "It's ringing."

They waited.

For a moment, the silence swirled around them. Then, just when Kaylee thought the call was not going to connect, a jangling melody started up, making them both jump.

Kaylee recognized it as the cheesy show tune Jeremy had selected for his ringtone. She'd begged him to change it more than once for something a little more current. A little less lame.

"He's not answering," Ben said in frustration as the phone stopped ringing and connected to voicemail.

Jeremy's voice, sounding thinner than in real life, coaxed them to leave a message.

"I can hear that, genius." Kaylee hung up before the prompt finished. "Where was it coming from?"

"I couldn't tell," Ben said. "Try again."

"Hang on." Kaylee redialed.

The jarring ringtone started up anew.

"Sounds like it's coming from up front," Ben said. "Out in the auditorium."

"I don't think so. It's closer." Kaylee took a step forward, following the sound. She reached the edge of the stage, her gaze sweeping across the rows of empty seats and dimly lit aisles, but she saw nothing. Then, at the same moment the phone clicked over to voicemail for a second time, she looked down into the darkened pit where the orchestra performed. It wasn't in use right now since their own show contained no musical numbers. The music stands and folding metal chairs used by the musicians were stacked to the sides, leaving the central area open and empty.

Only it wasn't empty. Not quite.

A figure lay sprawled across the hard concrete floor. A figure Kaylee recognized only too well despite his ruined face and the halo of dark blood seeping around his inert body. She lifted her hands to her face in horror and screamed.

THREE

NEWLY MINTED FBI Special Agent Patterson Blake entered the Istanbul Palace Lebanese Restaurant and Tavern in the Borough of Queens a little after seven in the evening and looked around the half-full dining room. She spied her father right away, standing at the bar sipping a bottle of beer.

When he saw her, his eyes lit up, and he walked her way. "Peanut, you made it."

"Did you think I wouldn't?" Patterson asked. His nickname for her, Peanut, was because of her initials. PB—as in peanut butter. It was something he'd been calling her ever since Patterson could remember.

"I don't know. It's been an eternity since I last saw you."

"It's been four months, Dad. Hardly that long." The air in the restaurant was redolent with the fragrance of Knefeh, a Middle Eastern cheese-filled sweet dessert, and Markouk, a delicious and delicate flatbread. It made Patterson's mouth water.

"A lifetime to me. You're all I have in this world." He led Patterson back to the bar. "Running off like you did on that silly obsession of yours and leaving me all alone."

"It's not a silly obsession. I was at Quantico training to be a federal law enforcement officer."

"Right. A cop." The elder Blake pulled a face. "Honestly, I don't know why you couldn't pick a safe profession. Something more—"

"More what?" Patterson motioned for the bartender and ordered a bottle of Almaza, a light Lebanese pilsner.

"You know." Her father shrugged.

"Feminine?"

"That wasn't what I was going to say. I'm not a Neanderthal. But running around with guns and chasing people... I swear if your mother were here to see—"

"Mom's not dead, Dad. She lives in Colorado." Patterson shook her head. "Can you try to be happy for me? This is a big deal. It's what I want to do."

"I am happy for you," her father said. "And proud, too. I know how much work it took to get into the FBI. Doesn't stop me worrying, though."

"I know." Patterson put her beer down on the counter. "Look, Dad. How about we enjoy tonight, and tomorrow I'll show you my new apartment."

Her father smiled. "I'd like that. Although you could have just come back home. It's not like I don't have the room."

"Dad..."

"Okay. I'm just saying . . ."

"I'm not a teenager anymore," Patterson said. "I think we both need our own space."

"You're probably right."

"Besides. I'll be on call all hours of day and night. An FBI agent is never really off duty. You're too set in your ways to put up with that."

"I agreed with you already, didn't I?" Her dad took another sip of his beer. "How about we enjoy our dinner, and I promise not to give you a hard time from here on out?"

"Sounds good to me." Patterson clinked her glass against her father's and took a sip of her own beer. And just like that, the tension dropped away. Patterson felt herself relax. The knot in her stomach released. She knew her father wasn't happy with her choice of career, and to tell the truth, she'd had mixed feelings about meeting him for dinner. They had always been close, but her dogged determination to join the FBI had tested that relationship over the last few years. She knew it worried him, and she felt bad for that, but it was her life, not his.

"So, how is the new job so far?" Her father asked. "And don't worry, I'm not going to start up again. I just want to know how long it will be before I can tell everyone my daughter is the director of the FBI."

Patterson laughed and shook her head. "You might have to wait awhile on that one. I've only been out of the Academy for a couple of weeks."

"Never hurts to have goals," her father said as a buzzer sitting on the bar went off. He glanced down. "Speaking of which, I believe our table is ready."

They picked up their drinks and were soon seated at a

table near the window. After ordering their meals, the elder Blake returned to the previous conversation. "All joking aside, how are you doing at the new job?"

"I'm doing good. It's been fun, if uneventful. A lot of early mornings. I've been on the range every morning before 7 AM doing firearms training, and there's a ton of desk work. I mean, *a ton*. But I went on a raid last week. The office of a Manhattan lawyer with mob ties. That was exciting. But the job isn't really like what you see on TV. We just walked in and showed a warrant, then took his computers away while the staff stood around and watched with their arms folded."

"Well, that sounds anticlimactic." Her father smiled. "Sounds like you didn't even get to kick down any doors."

"I'm fairly sure the door kicking is a small part of the job," Patterson said as their food came.

They ate with gusto, focusing mostly on the food. In between mouthfuls, they chatted sporadically, hopping from subject to subject. Afterward, when their server had cleared the plates away, her father reached into his coat pocket and withdrew an item wrapped in blue paper with yellow stripes.

He pushed it across the table toward her. "It's not wrapped as nice as I would have liked. I couldn't find any ribbon in the house."

"What's this?" Patterson asked, picking up the surprise package.

"A gift. I wanted to give it to you when you graduated from the academy, but . . ."

"I know. You had to work."

"I feel bad, is all. I should have been there to support you."

"Even if you don't like the idea of your daughter being a Fed."

"I never said that, and we agreed to change the subject, remember?"

"Sorry." Patterson picked up the gift and tugged at the wrapping. Beneath the layers of thin shiny paper was an ornate silver picture frame with a photograph inside. She recognized it right away. Her father standing in a river holding a fishing pole. He was flanked by a pair of girls. On one side was a twelve-year-old Patterson, with the same blond hair she still had now at twenty-four, except it was shorter in the picture. She stood proud with a tight grip on her own fishing pole. On the other side was her older sister, Julie, with a tackle box in her hand. Despite the smile on her face, she looked uncomfortable. Behind the camera, Patterson knew, was their mother. "Wow. I'd forgotten all about this trip. This was the year you took us to the Adirondacks and made us stay in that leaky tent you bought from Frank Clarke, who lived next door."

"Paradox Lake. You remember." Her father beamed.

"How could I forget? Julie spent the entire trip complaining about mosquitoes and worrying that we were going to get eaten by a bear. She hated camping so much."

"She hated fishing even more. I think the only time she got in the water with us was to pose for that picture."

"And then she made us take her back to the tent so she could change into dry clothes even though she hadn't really gotten wet. She was wearing waders."

"Which she never wore again after that day." Patterson's father laughed. "Should have listened to your mother and not bothered buying them. Could have spent the money on tackle instead."

"And then we wouldn't have this picture," Patterson said, smiling. She looked down at the photograph and the three of them together. "This was the last trip we all took together before she went to college."

"That's right, it was."

"I miss Julie." Patterson touched the frame, a tear pushing at the corner of her eye. "I miss her so much."

"Me too, Peanut." Her father's face creased in sadness, then he shook it off and forced a smile. "Heavens. I didn't mean to upset you with that pic. I just wanted to remind you that there are real people, families like us, behind every crime. That every case you solve could bring peace to someone in distress."

Patterson nodded. "That's why I joined the FBI."

"As long as you never forget."

"I won't." Patterson glanced at her watch. "Shoot. It's late, and I have to be up early tomorrow."

"In that case, we'd better get you home to that swanky new apartment." Her father raised his hand to get the check.

"Let me." Patterson reached for her purse.

"Nonsense. This is a celebration of your achievement. This one is on me. And then I'm walking you back to the subway."

"There's no need. Go on home. I can walk myself."

"Not happening. You might be a cop now, but these streets aren't safe, and you're still my daughter."

"Alright." Patterson knew better than to argue. "But only as far as the subway. And next time, I'm paying."

"Does that mean this is going to be a regular thing?"

"If you want it to be," Patterson said. "I'd like that."

"Me, too," the elder Blake said as the server brought their check. "But we're only eating in Queens. You know how I feel about Brooklyn."

"I do, although I can't fathom why." Patterson laughed.

"Too many hipsters." Her father dropped a wad of cash on the table to cover their meal, then stood up with a grunt. "Come on. Let's get you home."

FOUR

PATTERSON RODE the subway back to her apartment on the second floor of a brownstone in the Queens neighborhood of Astoria. It was late, and there was barely anyone on the train. The few other riders occupying the carriage never gave her a second glance. She got off at the Ditmars Boulevard station and walked the last couple of blocks to her apartment, passing her Bureau-assigned car parked up at the curb outside as she reached the building. The car was only to be used for official business, hence the need for Patterson to ride the train.

Patterson made her way inside the building and up to her apartment. She was tired and looking forward to a long, hot shower. She unlocked the front door and switched on the lights. As she stepped into the hallway, her phone rang. She grabbed it from her purse and looked at the incoming number. It was her new boss, Jonathan Grant. She tapped to answer and pressed the phone to her ear.

"Grant?" she said, sensing the chance of a hot shower slipping away. As an FBI agent, she was never truly off duty. A call could come at any time of day or night. Now her decision not to have a second beer with dinner seemed prudent, especially given her status as a newbie. "What can I do for you?"

"Special Agent Patterson." Grant's voice came across the line, sounding tired. "Where are you right now?"

"I'm at home. I was just about to take a quick shower and then climb into bed. Why?"

"Better grab a cup of coffee. Make it strong. You're going to be up a while longer. There's been a murder. You're back on the clock."

"Oh. Wow." Patterson realized the reply sounded odd as soon as she spoke, but this would be her first real crime scene. She felt a tingle of excitement, interlaced with apprehension. "Where do you need me?"

"Montauk. The Phoenix Theater on Main."

"Got it. My Bucar is right outside," Patterson said, using agency slang for the Bureau vehicle assigned to her the day she arrived at the New York Field Office, fresh out of Quantico. "Give me five minutes to grab that coffee, and I'll be on my way."

"Take ten," Grant said. "We'll ride together in my car. I'll swing by and pick you up. I'm already on my way out of the city. Driving over the Queensboro Bridge as we speak."

"Okay," Patterson said, surprised. "My address is—"

"I know where you live. I'll be there in less than fifteen."

"How—"

"I'm your supervisor. I know where all my agents live."

"Sorry." Patterson felt silly. "I'll be waiting when you get here."

"Perfect," Grant said. "And bring your go bag. You'll need it."

"We're staying overnight?" Patterson asked. All agents kept a bag packed with the necessities in their trunks. Officially called a go bag, it contained a couple of days' change of clothes and toiletries, extra high-capacity magazines and bullets for her Glock pistol, a Bureau baseball cap, the mandatory windbreaker with the letters FBI stenciled on the back in yellow, and handcuffs-both regular and flex. There was also a bulletproof vest. Her defense tactics instructor at Quantico had been vocal about the importance of this bag. She wondered why Grant wanted her to take it now. "We're only going to Montauk. We can just drive back when we're done."

"You ever drive on the Long Island Expressway?"

"Point taken." Patterson had grown up in Ozone Park and knew the LIE only too well. Catch it at the wrong time of day, and you might as well be in a parking lot. The road was notorious for congestion.

"Now, if you're done questioning my decision-making skills, I suggest you go make that coffee." There wasn't a hint of irritation in Grant's voice. If anything, he sounded amused. "I'll be outside your building in eleven minutes and thirty-four seconds, according to my GPS, and I expect you to be ready and waiting."

"Understood. See you outside." Patterson ended the call and returned the phone to her pocket. She lifted her hand to the slight bulge under her coat, checking that her Glock was still sitting in its shoulder harness, tucked snugly against her left rib cage, even though she knew it would be. She hurried to the bedroom and slipped out of the black skirt she'd been wearing, exchanging it for a pair of jeans. That done, she strapped an ankle holster containing a Glock 27 subcompact to her inside left leg. This was her backup weapon. She slipped the leg of her jeans down to conceal it and made her way to the kitchen, where she brewed coffee and poured it into a travel mug.

Then she was heading toward the door, turning the apartment lights back off as she went. Downstairs, she grabbed the go bag from the trunk of the Bureau car and was standing at the curb a full minute before Grant pulled up.

FIVE

"I DON'T GET IT. This seems like more of a job for the local boys," Patterson said as she rode in Jonathan Grant's car with her go bag behind her on the back seat. It was almost midnight, and the roads were dark and empty. They slid onto the Long Island Expressway and drove east toward Montauk. Grant had just finished briefing her. A murder at a local summer theater. The writer and director of a play opening the next week had been killed after he stayed behind after rehearsal to work on the show. Two members of the cast became worried and returned to see why he was taking so long to join them at a bar down the street, only to discover his bludgeoned corpse. "The FBI rarely inserts itself into cases like this so quickly. Don't we usually wait until our help is requested? Unless I'm mistaken."

"You're not," Grant said. He glanced sideways at her, green eyes catching the light from a streetlamp as they drove past. "But this is not a run-of-the-mill case. I'm sure you know who Marilyn Kahn is."

"Who doesn't?" Patterson replied. Marilyn Kahn was the Special Agent in Charge, or SAC for short, of the Criminal Investigative Division at the New York Field Office. She was both Patterson and Grant's boss. "What does she have to do with this?"

"Her sister, Aimee, is on the board of the theater," Grant told her. "Actually, she's the vice-chairman."

"I still don't see—" Patterson began before Grant cut her off.

"Kahn's family is old money. She grew up around the Hamptons. They wield a lot of power, and not just because Marilyn is shooting up the ranks at the FBI. Her father was a senator, as was her grandfather. Aimee is married to Clark Bradford. He's a founding partner in the law firm Gillibrand, Bradford, and Clarkson. They're prominent corporate lawyers with deep political ties in DC. They represent several political figures with influence over top positions at the Bureau. Many of these same politicians are involved in pet charitable projects."

"Like being patrons of the Phoenix Theater," Patterson said.

"Exactly. Marilyn senses an opportunity to get on their radar."

"Or maybe she just wants to help her sister?"

Grant chuckled. "Marilyn Kahn is ruthless in her ambition. Believe me, this is more about forging powerful ties than helping family."

"Ah. We're just showing up to be seen."

"On the contrary," Grant said. "I intend to investigate this murder as I would any other crime. Marilyn Kahn might be using us and the New York Field Office for her own ends, but that doesn't mean we shouldn't do our jobs."

"And how do the locals feel about us showing up out of the blue?"

"I can't imagine anyone will object." Grant glanced sideways toward Patterson; his face momentarily illuminated as they passed under a streetlamp before falling back into shadow. "We generally have a good relationship with local law enforcement. I'm sure they will be happy for the help."

"Probably." Patterson lapsed into silence for a few moments before speaking up again. "I'm curious. Why are you bringing me along?"

"Why not?" Grant turned his attention back to the road. "You are an FBI agent."

"Barely out of the Academy. There must be more qualified agents you could take. People with more experience in murder investigations."

"That's precisely why I chose you. It should be easy to wrap up, and you need to learn. Are you nervous?"

"A little," Patterson admitted. "My only fieldwork so far was that raid in Manhattan. It was kind of boring, to tell the truth."

"Welcome to the FBI," Grant said with a laugh. "It's less action hero than it is an office worker with a cool badge. When I got out of the Academy, it was three months before I took part in an active murder investigation. I was so nervous I thought I'd throw up."

"I'm not that bad," Patterson said with a grin.

"We'll see." Grant exited the expressway and turned right onto a road that would take them to State Highway 27. From there, it was a straight shot to Montauk. "Tell me, have you ever seen a dead body?"

"Sure. More than one," Patterson replied. "At the body farm."

"Not the same thing," Grant said. The body farm, officially called the Forensic Anthropology Center, was a facility in Knoxville, Tennessee. Using real cadavers donated in life by their erstwhile owners or the relatives of a recently deceased individual, the center provided law enforcement agencies such as the FBI with scene of crime training related to the collection of forensic evidence from bodies. "I mean a real murder victim."

"No, I haven't," Patterson admitted. "But how different can it be?"

"It's a world of difference," Grant said. "You're not dealing with a neatly placed corpse donated to science. This is a person who should still be alive. Someone whose life was snatched away from them without remorse. The violence is not staged. It's real, and it's visceral. Not everyone handles it well the first time."

Patterson lapsed into silence. She sat stiffly in her seat and stared through the passenger window, watching the dark scenery pass by. A tight knot of dread formed in her stomach, fueled by Grant's words. She didn't know what she would see in the next few hours, but she had a feeling it would change her outlook forever.

SIX

MONTAUK'S MAIN Street was a hive of activity, with police cruisers, a forensics unit, a mobile command post vehicle, and an ambulance all parked outside the Phoenix Theater, which should have been locked up and quiet at such an hour. Police lights danced across the surrounding buildings, bathing the entire scene in surreal tones of red and blue. A Suffolk County cruiser stood parked on each end of the block, next to hastily erected barricades being watched over by a uniformed officer.

When Grant pulled up and flashed his FBI credentials, the officer drew the barrier back and watched them proceed down the street and park opposite the theater next to a building that contained a cruise wear boutique and a Mediterranean restaurant.

Patterson climbed from the car. She stood waiting for Grant, her gaze wandering across the strange tableaux. A cluster of police officers talked on the sidewalk. An unmarked unit that surely belonged to a homicide detective was parked at an angle close to the theater doors with blue lights flashing inside its front grill. Two paramedics stood with arms folded, waiting to receive a patient long past any help they might render. A man in white coveralls emerged from an alley between the theater and the building next door, carrying what looked like a large toolbox. A forensic technician. He walked to a van and placed the toolbox inside, then turned and disappeared back into the alley.

"You ready to roll?" Grant asked, exiting the car and looking across the vehicle's roof toward her.

"Ready as I'll ever be," Patterson replied. She took a deep breath and rounded the front of the car, stepping off the sidewalk onto the road. As she did so, her gaze swept across the closed and dark Mediterranean restaurant to her right, and she thought absently that her father would like to eat there. He loved Greek food. She would need to remember it and suggest a trip down here one day. But right now, there was a murder to investigate. Patterson hurried to join Grant, and together they crossed to the theater and entered the alley, soon finding themselves at a stage door propped wide open with a brick.

A man in a crumpled suit stood in the doorway, with one hand pushed deep into his pocket and the other holding a cigarette stub. The shield hanging from his belt identified him as a detective. He looked tired, with dark bags under his eyes. Upon seeing Patterson and Grant, he pushed himself up straighter with some effort.

"You must be the G-man," he said, focusing on Grant and ignoring Patterson.

"We're with the FBI," Grant said, not bothering to hide his annoyance at the slight to Patterson. "Both of us."

"Right." The detective's eyes rolled sideways toward Patterson, then snapped back to Grant. He held his hand out. "Detective Ahlstrom. Suffolk County Homicide."

"Supervisory Special Agent Jonathan Grant. My partner is Special Agent Patterson Blake."

"Pleased to make your acquaintances," Ahlstrom said without enthusiasm. The detective licked his lips and glanced over his shoulder toward the theater interior, then back to the agents again. "Suppose you want me to show you the scene."

"That would be nice," Grant replied.

Ahlstrom nodded but didn't move to let them in. Instead, he stepped aside to allow a forensics tech to exit the building, then resumed his position blocking the door. "You know, for the life of me, I can't figure out what y'all are doing here."

"We're just following orders, same as you," Grant said.

"Yeah. Except right now, all you're doing is gumming up the works. We've been ready to move the body for twenty minutes, but the powers that be told us we had to wait for the pair of you. Either there's a federal angle to this that we haven't been informed about, or someone is looking to snag a slice of glory out of tragedy."

Grant shrugged. "I wouldn't know anything about that."

"The sooner you let us see the crime scene, the quicker you can move the body," Patterson said, stepping forward into the detective's line of sight. "Unless your cigarette break isn't over yet."

Ahlstrom watched her for a moment, his eyes narrowing, then he turned and retreated into the building, gesturing for them to follow. "Come on then, let's get this over with."

As they entered, Grant leaned close to Patterson so that his mouth was close to her ear and spoke in a half-whisper. "Nice job putting that guy in his place."

"My pleasure," Patterson said, unable to suppress a thin smile.

If the detective heard, he made no show of it. Instead, he led the two FBI agents backstage. They passed a room with a sign on the door that read *costume*, overloaded with racks of clothes. Beyond these, she saw several sewing machines and a large table covered in bolts of fabric. Moving on, they arrived at a set of concrete steps leading down into the bowels of the theater. Patterson glanced at the costume room and its contents as she passed, then followed Grant and Ahlstrom down the steps.

They traversed a short corridor with dressing rooms on each side and came to a door through which Patterson could see a woman in white coveralls stenciled with the letters CSI and a couple of uniformed cops. A photographer lingered in the hallway near the door with a digital SLR slung around his neck. A ring flash circled the lens. He flattened himself against the wall to allow them to pass.

The female crime scene technician glanced up at their approach, then turned away, her attention focused downward toward the floor.

Ahlstrom reached the doorway and stopped, standing aside for Grant and Patterson to enter.

"Better brace yourselves, this is nasty," he said in a grave voice as they drew level with him.

The room beyond the door was not what Patterson expected. A low ceiling overhung the first half of the space, while the rest was open. The far wall was only half-height. Beyond it, she could see rows of chairs disappearing up into the darkness, and further away, a second level curving around atop the first. The theater auditorium. She realized they were standing in the orchestra pit.

It was lit by dim overhead lights affixed to the half ceiling, which Patterson now realized was the apron for the stage above. Adding to this and flooding everything in brilliant white light were halogen lamps standing on tripods. These had been set up by the forensics team. But it was what the lamps illuminated that made her stop in her tracks.

A man's body.

He lay sprawled on the hard concrete floor, surrounded by a dark lake of viscous fluid that Patterson knew was blood. She looked at the corpse, at first unable to process what she was seeing, but then the true horror of the scene in front of her clicked into place. The man's face was missing, cratered in until all that was left was a bloodied concave pulp. She felt the bile rising in her throat. Felt her chest tighten. Then Patterson stumbled backward out of the room and fled back down the corridor, not stopping until she reached the foot of the steps leading up to the stage door through which they had entered the building. Behind her, Detective Ahlstrom snickered.

SEVEN

PATTERSON STOPPED at the bottom of the steps and drew in several long breaths. Her heart was racing, and she thought she might throw up, but after a minute the worst of it subsided.

"You okay there, partner?"

She looked around and saw Grant hurrying toward her, a concerned look on his face. She nodded. "I'm fine. Just got caught off guard, is all."

"Hey, no need to apologize. Happens to the best of us." Grant closed in on her and came to a stop a few feet away. "The minute something like that stops affecting you, it's time to get out of the game."

"It was unprofessional."

"Nah." Grant shook his head. "It was honest."

"Is that how Detective Ahlstrom viewed it?" Patterson clenched her fists when she thought about the detective laughing at her reaction.

"Screw him." Grant took a step closer. He raised an eyebrow. "You really care what that jackass thinks?"

"No," Patterson admitted. "But I care about doing my job without freaking out."

"You remember what I told you earlier?" Grant asked. "In the car on the way here."

"About the body farm not being like real life?"

"Exactly." Grant leaned against the wall and folded his arms. "Do you think you're the only newbie to balk at the sight of their first homicide victim?"

"Probably." Patterson was mad at herself, as much as anything. She wanted to prove she could handle the job, and instead ended up running like a scared schoolgirl.

"Well, you're not. I've seen men three times your size turn tail on their first homicide investigation. It's normal. If you weren't shocked by this, I'd think there was something wrong with you."

"You're just trying to make me feel better."

"I can assure you, that's the last thing I'm doing," Grant said. "If I thought you couldn't handle it in the field, I'd pass that information on up the line, and you'd be gone. This isn't that. It's a normal human reaction to the brutal reality of a violent crime scene. You'll get better at controlling it, but the outrage you feel at the taking of another human life proves you have compassion. Don't ever let that slip away."

"I'll do my best." Patterson didn't think she would ever be able to look at a crime scene like the one they had just walked into without a deep sense of tragedy, but at the same time, she needed to be better at managing her reaction. She pulled herself together and looked at Grant. "We should go back in there."

"You sure about that?" Grant observed her with narrowed eyes. "I can handle this bit if you need more time."

"No." Patterson stepped away from the stairs back in the direction of the orchestra pit. "I'm not giving that moron detective the satisfaction of thinking he's right about me. I'm doing this."

"Good for you." Grant smiled and walked at her side as they made their way back along the corridor.

When they arrived at the door to the pit, Ahlstrom was blocking the way. He turned around. A flicker of surprise—or maybe it was badly concealed annoyance—flashed across his face.

"You back for more, little lady?" He asked, the corners of his mouth curling into a faint sneer. His eyes shifted to Grant. "Glutton for punishment, am I right?"

"Special Agent Blake is doing her job," Grant replied, his own tone leaving no doubt regarding his opinion of the detective's words. "And right now, you're obstructing that."

"Well, pardon me. I'll just step aside to let the horse see the cart." Ahlstrom pushed between the two agents, his body pressing into Patterson in the narrow corridor as he did so.

She caught a whiff of garlic on his breath and turned her head away, sucking her chest in against the unwelcome and intrusive contact.

With the doorway now clear, Grant motioned for Patterson to lead the way back into the pit.

Her reaction to the victim was just as visceral the second

time around as it had been the first, but now she was expecting it, and swallowed the wave of horror that swept over her when she looked at the corpse.

"What do you think?" Grant asked, coming up behind her and placing a calming hand on her elbow. "First impressions?"

"Obviously, this man was murdered. Bludgeoned to death by a blunt instrument," Patterson said, indicating the ruined face that now stared lifelessly up from the one eye that was still identifiable. Her gaze slipped from the body to an object lying in the blood nearby. A heavy-duty claw hammer. "And I guess we don't need to look far for the murder weapon."

"And?" Grant prodded.

"This is a crime of passion. The perp could have dispatched their victim with no more than a few blows given the weight of that hammer, yet the killer kept going until the face was all but obliterated. The victim would have been dead before even half this damage was done. The skull isn't just cracked, it's smashed. One side of this man's head has been reduced to mush."

"So, what does that tell you?"

"Our aggressor was full of rage at the time of the incident," Patterson said, succinctly summing up her observation of the crime scene. "I would be surprised if our victim startled an intruder or if this was a simple robbery gone wrong. The perpetrator meant to kill this man. Came here for that purpose. Even if the actual murder wasn't premeditated, the intention to harm absolutely was. I would theorize there's a personal connection between the victim and the perp."

"Very good." Grant nodded. "I was thinking the same thing. Most murders are committed by people known to the victim, especially when there are indicators of strong emotion involved."

"A co-worker or family member?" Patterson said. "Someone who knew he would be here alone. Knew his habits."

"That's a good place to start." Grant turned to the detective, who was leaning against the wall in the corridor with an unlit cigarette between his fingers. "Where is the young woman who called this in?"

"Not here," Ahlstrom said. "We released her, and she went home. In a hell of a state. Barely got her to calm down enough to give a statement. The guy she was with is gone too."

"You let them leave?" Grant asked, incredulous. "How do you know they weren't involved?"

The detective shrugged. "We have their home addresses. If the evidence leads us to believe either one is a suspect, we can bring them in."

"And if they don't stick around for that?"

"Relax. They didn't do it."

"And how do you know that?"

"Because I can read people. I'm a good judge of character. Been doing this job a long time."

"Yeah." Grant took a business card with the FBI seal printed on the front from his pocket and handed it to Ahlstrom. "My cell number and email address are both on this card. When you get a moment, please send me their statements."

"Sure, when I have time." The detective reached out and took the card, then folded it and shoved it into his pocket. "Might be a while. I have a crime scene to work."

"Tonight, if you don't mind," Grant replied. "And while you're at it, you can email me the crime scene photos."

"You want me to fetch you a couple cups of coffee, too?" Ahlstrom asked, his eyes turning dark. "Since I'm running around after you all."

"No." Grant was unphased by the sarcasm. "But I do want the coroner's report the moment you have it." He turned to Patterson. "Come on, let's get out of here."

"Really? We've barely gotten here." Patterson glanced toward the body. "You don't want to stay and investigate the scene?"

"The detective appears to have it all under control," Grant replied. He looked at Ahlstrom. "Isn't that right?"

"Sure."

"There you go." Grant turned his attention back to Patterson but made sure the detective heard his words. "And he'll keep us apprised of any new information or pertinent leads, I'm sure."

The detective nodded but said nothing.

Grant almost smiled but then pulled it back. "See? We aren't needed here. Let's go find a place to lay our heads. It's late, and I'm tired." With that, he turned and strode back along the corridor.

Patterson glanced back at the body, felt her stomach clench again, then tore her eyes away. Recovering her composure, she removed one of her own business cards and held it out to the detective.

"You can copy me in, too," she said with all the authority she could muster.

Ahlstrom snatched it from her hand. "I'll see what I can do."

"Good," Patterson replied with a measure of satisfaction, then she turned and hurried after her partner.

EIGHT

WHAT THEY FOUND WAS a motel out by the highway. It was much like other cheap off-the-interstate motels Patterson had stayed in over the years. A two-story building with a balcony that ran along its front facade, and a small office sitting out front near the road. A neon sign hanging in the office window advertised color TV—as if any modern accommodation didn't provide such a basic amenity—and announced that there were vacancies.

Grant took care of the rooms, leaving Patterson in the car while he went inside the office, then returned five minutes later and climbed back into the car before handing her a flat plastic keycard.

"Room eleven," he said, putting the car in gear and rolling forward through the parking lot before pulling into a space outside a room near the middle of the hotel block with an air conditioner that was depositing too much water onto the sidewalk. "I'm in twelve, next door."

"I hope the rooms are nicer inside than they look from out here," Patterson said, peering through the windshield.

"I wouldn't hold your breath."

"You know how to show a girl a good time."

"So I've been told," Grant replied with a chuckle. "It's only for a night or two. Besides, you'd better get used to crappy hotel rooms. The FBI per diem is hardly generous."

"I've heard that." Patterson pulled her door open and climbed out of the car, then reached into the back seat and grabbed her go bag. "I guess it's true."

"I've stayed in worse," Grant said, slamming the driver's door and going to the trunk to retrieve his own bag. A minute later, he joined her on the sidewalk outside their hotel rooms. "You need anything else tonight?"

"I'm good," Patterson replied. She pressed her key card against the reader and opened the door when the light turned green. "I think I'll sleep like a log tonight."

"Don't forget to set an alarm." Grant watched her step into the room and then leaned against the door frame. "I want to be up and at it early tomorrow. The first twenty-four hours is crucial and the less time we waste, the better."

"Sure." Patterson placed her bag on the closer of two full-size beds and turned to look at her boss. "What time?"

"Seven work for you?"

"Does it matter if I say no?"

"Not really."

"Seven it is, then."

"Great." Grant pushed himself up and turned to leave. "Sleep tight."

"You, too." Patterson watched her boss depart, her eyes

lingering on his retreating figure just a little longer than they should. He was handsome, with short-cropped dark hair and deep green eyes. Then she closed the door and returned to her overnight bag. She unzipped it and reached inside, withdrawing the silver frame her father had given her earlier at the restaurant. Her eyes lingered on the photograph within. The two Blake sisters and their dad fishing as if they didn't have a care in the world. The memories of that last trip together came flooding back and she smiled, before the reality of what happened afterward crashed down upon her. She pushed the memory away and set the frame down on the nightstand, then grabbed her toiletries bag and headed for the bathroom.

Ten minutes later, now dressed in a T-shirt and shorts, Patterson sat on the edge of the bed, phone in hand. She fired off a quick text message to let her father know she wouldn't be around for a few days, then ended it by saying she loved him. She placed the phone on the nightstand next to the silver frame, and once again found herself staring at the photograph within. Patterson's gaze lingered on her sister for a moment. She reached out and touched the glass as if the gesture could span the gulf of time that separated them, then mouthed a silent good night before climbing into bed and turning out the lights. Patterson was asleep less than a minute later.

NINE

GRANT KNOCKED on Patterson's door at 7 AM sharp.

She was already up and dressed, thanks to some inconsiderate jerks on the floor above who woke her by repeatedly slamming their hotel room door as they came and went with what sounded like heavy luggage.

Knowing she wouldn't get back to sleep, Patterson had risen and made use of the time to get some work done. Detective Ahlstrom had emailed the crime scene photos and witness statements to Grant and copied her in. She saw nothing new in the photographs but read through the statements twice. If she was expecting to find a motive for murder somewhere in the words, there wasn't one. By the time Grant arrived, she was browsing the internet looking for information on Jeremy Knight, their victim.

When she opened the door, Grant was on the other side clutching two drinks in paper cups with plastic lids.

"The coffee in the room was gross, and I mean seriously

dreadful, so I ran down the road to a Starbucks I saw last night when we were driving here," he said, stepping into the room. "I probably should've called and asked what you wanted, but I figured you'd still be sleeping."

"Not a chance," Patterson said, taking the coffee Grant offered her. "Too much noise up above."

"Woke you too, huh?"

"You'd think people would have a little more consideration when they're staying in a hotel like this." Patterson returned to her laptop and sat back down. She placed the coffee on the table next to her computer and pulled the plastic lid off. A wisp of steam trapped beneath wafted up into the air. "I don't suppose you brought milk or sugar?"

"Sure did." Grant put his own coffee down and pushed a hand into his pocket. He came out with an assortment of sugar packets and single-serve creamer cups in various flavors. "I didn't know how you take your coffee, so I grabbed a bunch of everything."

"Ooh, vanilla." Patterson snatched up a creamer and ripped the lid off, then dumped it into her coffee. She looked up at Grant, who was still standing. "What's on the agenda today, boss?"

"First thing I want to do is talk to that pair of actors who discovered the body. Kaylee Robinson and Ben Ford." Grant finally took the other seat and leaned with his elbows on the table. He sipped his coffee black, ignoring the creamer and sugar. A smile touched his lips. "Definitely better than the slop in my room."

"Detective Ahlstrom sent their statements already," Patterson said, nodding toward the computer. "I just skimmed through them, and nothing piqued my interest. Do we really need to talk to the actors again?"

"Absolutely." Grant peered at Patterson over the top of her laptop. "I always like to interview witnesses personally. You lose so much with a written report. Like how the witness reacts when you ask questions. Body language is important. It can let you know if someone is hiding something or lying. It can also give valuable insight into their mental state. Besides, if you go by the report, you're limited to whatever the interviewer asked. You might have better questions of your own. Questions that could break the case."

"Sorry, I should have known that already," Patterson said, chiding herself for not thinking before she spoke. Her instructor at Quantico had said much the same thing during her classes on interview technique.

"Don't fret it. I brought you along on this investigation to gain field experience," Grant said. He nodded toward the computer. "Looks like you've been doing some research already. What did you find out?"

"A whole heap of nothing much." Patterson closed the laptop. "Jeremy Knight was the director, writer, and male lead in the show they were rehearsing last night. He also founded the theater company staging the play."

"Not a humble man, then."

"Apparently not. His bio on the theater company website said he teaches drama at a local community college. Before that, he had some minor roles on Broadway and did a couple of touring productions up and down the East Coast. He's married and lives… sorry, lived… locally. I couldn't find much else on him."

"Uh-huh." Grant nodded. "I did some digging of my own this morning. Ran his name through NCIC."

"Anything?" Patterson asked. NCIC, or the National Crime Information Center, was a national database maintained by the FBI that allowed police agencies country wide to check arrest warrants and criminal convictions, among other things. It wasn't perfect because local and State information sometimes didn't make it into the system. But it was a good starting point.

Grant shook his head. "Nada."

"So he doesn't have a record, so far as we know," Patterson said.

"If he does, it's not in NCIC. I also checked with Detective Ahlstrom this morning before I went for coffee."

"That must have gone down well," Patterson said, glancing at the time on the nightstand clock.

"He can get his beauty sleep after we solve this." Grant sounded pleased with himself. "But you're right. He wasn't happy to hear from me."

"And?"

"Suffolk County PD hasn't encountered him before, either."

"If the locals don't have anything, then he's probably clean."

"Right. Not even a parking ticket. It's a shame. I was hoping something would stand out. A reason why someone would want him dead."

"And someone clearly wanted him dead." An image of Jeremy Knight's corpse, head nothing but a bloody pulp next to the hammer that killed him, entered Patterson's mind.

"People don't beat you like that unless you've really pissed them off."

"Agreed." Grant sighed and downed the last of his coffee. He stood and threw the empty cup into a small plastic trashcan several feet away with perfect aim, then he turned toward the door. "You ready to go solve a murder?"

"Ready and willing," Patterson replied. She went to the second bed, the one she wasn't sleeping in, and grabbed a gray leather jacket from beside her travel bag. It was May, but the weather could go either way. It might be seventy degrees one day and fifty-five the next. This morning, ash gray clouds blocked the sun, and Patterson suspected it might rain. When she turned around, Grant was already out the door. She pulled her jacket on, made sure her gun was securely in its shoulder holster, then scooped up her key card and followed him.

TEN

THEY DROVE into town and followed the directions from Grant's GPS until they arrived at the apartment complex where Ben Ford, one of the two actors who discovered Jeremy Knight's body, currently lived. They pulled into a parking space next to an air conditioning van with rust creeping around the wheel arches and climbed an exterior staircase to a second-floor unit with a bicycle leaning outside, chained to the balcony railings.

There were four doors in the narrow breezeway. Grant used his phone to double-check the email Detective Ahlstrom had sent and make sure they were in the right location, then rapped twice on the door marked 1203 with his knuckles.

They waited.

Nobody answered.

Grant knocked again, harder this time.

Still nothing.

He called the number Detective Ahlstrom had given him for Ben Ford, but it went to voicemail. He left a message and slipped the phone back into his pocket.

"I guess no one's home," Patterson said. "What now?"

"We wait to see if—" Grant stopped when a door across the breezeway opened.

An older woman with a cane and a pink bathrobe hanging open to reveal a flimsy nightgown came out of unit 1201.

"Can I help you?" the woman asked with narrowed eyes full of suspicion.

Grant took out his FBI credentials and held them up for her to see. "Mrs., uh . . ."

"Porter," the woman said.

"Mrs. Porter, we're looking for Ben Ford, but he doesn't seem to be home right now. Have you seen him recently?"

"Don't be so formal. Call me Fiona."

"Thank you," Grant said. "So, have you seen him?"

Fiona Porter snorted. "Him? Not since he stumbled in around one in the morning. Drunk as a skunk, I might add. Woke me up trying to get his key in the lock. I helped the poor lad inside just so I could get back to my warm bed." She shook her head and tutted. "It really isn't like him. He's always such a nice boy. Helps me up the stairs with my groceries. I didn't know what to make of it until I saw the news this morning. He's an actor, you know. A good one too. I went to see a play he was in a while back. Apparently, someone murdered his director last night after their rehearsal. No wonder he went and got himself soused. Must've been quite a shock."

"That's why we're looking for him," Grant said, slipping the credentials back into his pocket. "Have you seen Ben since helping him into the apartment?"

"You don't think he…" A look of horror passed across Fiona Porter's face. She reached out and steadied herself against the doorframe.

"Goodness, no." Patterson jumped in. "He's not a suspect at this time. We just want to speak with him about last night, that's all. Routine inquiries. Nothing to worry about."

"Oh." The fear drained from her face. "That's such a relief. I'd hate to think I was living across the hall from a killer."

"We understand," Grant said. "Have you seen him again since last night?"

The old woman shook her head. "Not seen him. But I heard him leave."

"When?" Patterson asked.

"About an hour ago." Fiona pulled the bathrobe around her narrow frame and shivered. "He left and hasn't come back since. Must have a hell of a headache after the way he came home, too."

"Any idea where he might've gone or when he'll return?"

"What do I look like, his secretary?" The old woman grimaced.

"That's a no, then," Patterson said.

"She's a quick one, huh?" The old woman looked at Grant.

"When you helped him into the apartment last night, did

you notice anything out of the ordinary?" Grant asked, ignoring the comment.

"You mean other than his being drunk? No." Fiona Porter shook her head. "Goodness. I hope he's alright."

Grant reached into his pocket and took out a business card. He handed it to the old woman. "When he returns, will you call us?"

"Sure." Fiona shrugged. "But I doubt he'll be back any time soon. When I heard him leave, I glanced out my bedroom window. It overlooks the parking lot. He took his bicycle and rode off with a bag on his back. The kind you take when you're going somewhere."

"He rode off?" Grant asked, glancing at the bicycle chained to the railings outside the actor's apartment. "This isn't his bike?"

"That one belongs to his roommate."

"Then why isn't the roommate answering the door?" Patterson asked. "Since his bike is here."

"Oh, Colin isn't at home either. He left about fifteen minutes before you showed up. He's an actor too, but he has a day job."

"He left on foot?"

"Nah. Sometimes he gets picked up by a car, so he doesn't need the bike. Today was one of those times. I assume it's a coworker giving him a ride."

"You know where he works?"

Fiona shook her head thoughtfully. "Sorry. He told me, but I forget. He's changed jobs a few times. Never seems to last long anywhere, so I pay little heed."

"You have a surname for this Colin fellow?"

"Langley. Colin Langley."

"Thanks," Patterson made a note of the name on her phone. She glanced at Grant. "I guess there's no point sticking around here any longer."

"Right. Maybe Ben will return my call." Grant stepped toward the stairs, then looked back at the old woman. "You've been very helpful, Fiona."

"I do what I can."

"If we think of anything else, we'll come back."

Fiona Porter observed them with watery eyes. "I'll be here. It's not like I have anyplace better to go."

"Thank you for taking the time to talk to us," Patterson said, stepping past the woman.

Grant started down the stairs.

Patterson followed, aware of Fiona Porter's gaze upon her back. When they reached the parking lot, she hurried to keep up with Grant. "You want to go looking for the roommate?"

"Not yet." Grant unlocked the car and slipped behind the wheel. He waited for Patterson to climb in before speaking again. "Kaylee Robinson doesn't live far from here. I want to talk to her next. She is, after all, the person who found Jeremy Knight's body in that orchestra pit. Maybe she knows more than she told the detective."

"You think she's hiding something?"

"I think Detective Ahlstrom was too busy making assumptions to ask the right questions." Grant started the car and reversed out of the parking space. He cast a glance sideways at Patterson. "I don't intend to make the same mistake."

ELEVEN

PATTERSON AND GRANT arrived at Kaylee Robinson's address ten minutes after leaving Ben Ford's apartment complex. The house was a small white single-story bungalow with a long thin yard in front surrounded by a picket fence. The lawn was badly in need of a mow, and weeds choked the flowerbeds.

"I guess Kaylee isn't much of a gardener," Grant said as they made their way up the path. When they reached the front door, he pressed the bell and waited.

"Just keep your fingers crossed that she's home," Patterson said. "Otherwise, our entire morning will be a bust."

"There's someone at home," Grant replied as a deadbolt drew back.

The door opened, and a young woman appeared. She was in her mid-twenties with shoulder-length brown hair highlighted with blue streaks, olive eyes, and a pale complexion. Patterson guessed her to be around five feet four inches tall and skinny. She probably didn't even weigh a hundred and ten pounds wet. She wore a white t-shirt with the words 'I'm done being your fool' printed across the front. Tight blue jeans clung to her legs.

She looked them up and down. "What do you want?"

"Are you Kaylee Robinson?" Patterson asked.

The girl let out a sigh. "No. Who are you guys?"

"My name is Special Agent Patterson Blake. This is my associate, Special Agent Jonathan Grant. We're with the FBI." Patterson showed her credentials, and Grant followed suit.

"FBI? Really?" The girl looked alarmed. "Is this about what happened at the theater?"

Patterson nodded. "What's your name?"

"Amber. I'm Kaylee's friend. She was in a state last night, so I stayed over."

"Is Kaylee here now?" Patterson asked.

"Yes," Amber replied. "She's still asleep."

"Can we speak with her?" Patterson asked. "It's important."

"Sure. Come on in." Amber held the door open and ushered them inside. "I'll go get Kaylee."

As Grant shut the front door behind him, Patterson cast an eye over their surroundings. Beyond a small, bare hallway was a lounge area with two sofas placed on either side of a fireplace with a brick mantle. A laptop sat open on the coffee table. Musical theater posters covered the walls. Patterson recognized several Broadway shows.

"What's your favorite musical?" Grant asked as they stepped into the room.

Patterson couldn't help a smile. "Really? My favorite musical?"

Grant shrugged. "I'll tell you mine if you tell me yours."

"You don't strike me as much of a theater person."

"You'd be surprised." Grant studied the posters.

"Well, in that case, my favorite musical is Cats."

"Really?" Grant smirked. "You like Cats?"

Patterson nodded. "Don't judge me. Your turn."

"Nah. Maybe later."

"Hey, not fair. We had a deal. No stalling."

Grant turned back to face the posters on the wall. "Alright, you got me. I hate musicals. All that singing for no reason. Gives me the creeps."

"You tricked me," Patterson said with mock outrage, but she couldn't help grinning.

"Yeah. Little bit." Grant's eyes flashed with mischief. "Cats! I thought you'd at least pick something from this millennium."

"That's the last time I'm telling you anything."

"We'll see," Grant said as the sound of footsteps echoed from the hallway.

They turned to see a slender blonde girl in pajamas standing in the doorway. There was no sign of the other girl, Amber.

"Are you Kaylee?" Patterson asked.

The girl nodded. "Yes, I'm Kaylee."

Patterson showed her creds again. "Special Agent Patterson Blake and Special Agent Jonathan Grant. We're with the FBI."

Kaylee looked at them with a mixture of surprise and fear. "Is this about last night?"

Patterson nodded. "We just have a few questions."

"I already gave a statement to the detective."

"We know, and we won't keep you long. I'm sure you're still shaken up."

Kaylee nodded mutely.

Grant stepped forward with his phone in hand. He had the statement Kaylee had given the night before up on the screen. He skimmed through it for a moment, then looked up at the nervous girl. "I just want to confirm what you said last night if that's okay."

"Sure." Kaylee crossed the room and sat on the edge of the closest sofa with her hands in her lap. "You want to sit down?"

"No. Thank you. I'd prefer to stand," Grant said. He scrolled through the witness statement a second time, then turned his attention back to Kaylee, questioning her at length. As she answered, he tapped notes into his phone, nodding occasionally.

Patterson studied the girl's face. She looked tired, with dark circles under her eyes. Freckles dotted her cheeks, and her blonde hair fell around her shoulders in gentle curling waves. There was something fragile about her that made Patterson think of a porcelain doll.

Grant went through the previous night's witness statement with the young woman. When he was satisfied, he pushed the phone back into his pocket and observed Kaylee for a long moment before asking, "How well did you know Jeremy Knight?"

"I don't know. Well enough. I was in his show, after all." Kaylee looked up at the two FBI agents. "Does it matter?"

"Just trying to get a handle on what occurred last night. You did, after all, go back to the theater looking for him."

"He was supposed to follow us to the pub once he'd finished working on the play. I got worried." Kaylee's forehead creased. "You know that already. I told it to the detective and confirmed it to you again a few minutes ago."

"Just making sure I understand." Grant folded his arms. "One more question, and then we'll leave you in peace."

"Sure." Kaylee nodded.

"Can you think of anyone who had a grudge against Jeremy Knight? Anyone who might want to hurt him?"

"Jeremy was the sweetest man," Kaylee said, wiping tears from her eyes. "He didn't deserve to die like that."

"That doesn't answer our question," Patterson said.

"Sorry." Kaylee sniffed. "I guess maybe his wife. They're going through a divorce. She's being a real bitch."

"Is that so?" Patterson exchanged a glance with Grant.

"She's been causing all sorts of trouble. He barely scraped together the money to put the show on. She wouldn't give him permission to use any joint funds even though she knew how much it means… meant to him."

"Do you know why they were getting divorced?" Patterson asked.

Kaylee shook her head. "I didn't want to pry."

"Thank you, Kaylee," Grant said. "You've been very helpful."

"My pleasure." Kaylee rubbed a meandering tear from

her cheek. "Do you think you'll catch the person who did this?"

"That's what we're paid to do," Grant replied reassuringly. He turned to leave, then hesitated, looking back at the young actress. "Actually, I do have another quick question. Are you acquainted with Ben Ford's roommate, Colin?"

"Yes. I know him. We hang out sometimes, all three of us. He's nice."

"I don't suppose you know where he works?"

"Actually, I do. Joe Mugs. The coffee shop on Main."

"Thank you again." Grant turned back toward the door.

Kaylee's friend Amber stood watching them from the kitchen. Grant met her gaze. "Take care of your friend, okay?"

Amber mouthed a silent acknowledgment.

Grant cast a quick look back into the living room and toward the girl sitting hunched on the sofa, then stepped outside with Patterson right behind.

TWELVE

JOE MUGS COFFEE shop occupied a storefront three blocks from the theater where the murder had taken place. When Grant and Patterson entered, the heady aroma of coffee and pastries filled their nostrils. A wall of windows provided a view of the street. Customers occupied the three small round tables in a row behind those windows. More tables filled the center of the room, around which customers sat tapping away at laptops or talking in hushed tones while sipping beverages from white ceramic mugs. A long counter ran along an exposed brick wall at the back of the coffee shop. The hiss of espresso machines filled the air, while classical music played through speakers set near the ceiling. Two servers worked behind the counter. One male, one female. They were both in their early twenties.

Patterson and Grant made a beeline for the male server, who was working the espresso machine.

"Colin Langley?" Grant asked, stepping up to the

counter and leaning forward to peer around the espresso machine.

"Hang on, man. Kinda in the middle of something here." Colin finished making the drink and handed it off to the other employee, who delivered it to the far end of the counter where a customer was waiting. That done, he turned to the two agents. "What can I get for you guys? I recommend the Café con Miele. It's flavored with honey, cinnamon, nutmeg, and vanilla. Really good."

"We're not here for the coffee," Grant said.

Colin shrugged, "Tea, then?"

"We're federal agents," Patterson said. "We want to ask you some questions about Ben Ford."

"What's he done?" A grin broke out on Colin's face.

"Nothing, so far as we know." Patterson felt like they weren't getting anywhere with their inquiries. This was the third place they had visited so far this morning, and the only new information they had uncovered was about the victim's impending divorce. While certainly a motive, the ferocity of the attack left her wondering. If the wife hated Jeremy Knight that much, why bother filing for divorce before committing murder? "You know Ben's whereabouts?"

"Sure. He's gone to the city. Won't be back for a couple of days."

"Mind elaborating?" Grant asked.

"You sure you guys don't want a coffee?" Colin looked between the two agents. "If I'm talking to you, I'm not making money. I pretty much work for tips."

"Fine, I'll take a latte," Grant said. "None of that nutmeg and vanilla stuff though."

"I'll take one too," Patterson said.

"That's more like it."

Colin busied himself making the coffees, talking as he did so. "Ben had an audition today for an off-Broadway show. He left early this morning. He was supposed to be coming back this afternoon because of the play, but it doesn't look like that will be going ahead now, considering."

"He'll be back later today?"

"No. Not anymore. Like I said, he was going to come back, so that he wouldn't miss rehearsal. But with the play all up in the air, he decided to stay in New York a few days longer and hit up some more auditions. He's crashing on a friend's couch. I don't know when he'll be coming back now."

"You have an address for this place he's staying?" Grant asked.

"No. I don't know the guy he's staying with. I think it's somewhere in Harlem if that's any help."

"Great. That narrows it down," Grant said. He pulled a twenty from his wallet and dropped it on the counter. "For the coffees. You can keep the change."

"Thanks, man." Colin scooped the bill up. "Much appreciated."

Patterson handed the barista her card. "That tip wasn't free. We need you to call us when Ben Ford comes back. It's important."

"Whatever you say." Colin took the card and slipped it into his apron pocket. "You sure he's not in trouble?"

"No. We're just crossing T's and dotting I's." Grant picked up his coffee. "This smells good."

"It is," Colin said. "Roast our own beans in-house."

"In that case, we might be back," Patterson said.

Colin grinned and leaned his elbows on the counter, eyes fixed upon Patterson. "Come back anytime. I'll make you my special frappé. Secret recipe."

"Does that offer extend to both of us or just my partner?" Grant asked, noticing how Colin was looking at Patterson.

"I guess I can make it for the pair of you," Colin said. "It's all good."

Patterson pushed her hands into her pockets, deliberately letting her jacket crease open to reveal the Glock in its shoulder holster. "That was the right answer, Colin. The right answer."

THIRTEEN

IT MIGHT BE bad luck to talk ill of the dead, but Jeremy was a cheating, lowlife scumbag." Linda Knight sat across from Grant and Patterson in her office at Island Realty, where the two FBI agents had tracked her down after they left the coffee shop. Detective Ahlstrom had already been there earlier that morning, and she wasn't happy about being interviewed for the second time in one day, but grudgingly agreed to give them ten minutes before she had to rush out to a showing on the other side of town. "If you want to know what I think, the enraged father of some impressionable young woman he was fooling around with probably murdered my husband."

"Is that why you filed for divorce?" Patterson asked. "Because Jeremy was fooling around with a girl at the college where he works?"

"Where he worked. Past tense." Linda scowled. "He

went and got himself fired a couple of months ago. Couldn't keep his hands off the female students."

"It must've been awful, finding out he was cheating like that."

"I already knew long before he got fired. I found a phone in his pocket when I was doing the laundry one day. A phone I'd never seen before. There were text messages on it between him and this girl. When I confronted him about it, he promised to stop and break it off. Like a fool, I believed him. A few weeks later, I dropped by the college to bring him some dinner because he was working late grading papers… or so I thought."

"I'm guessing he wasn't grading papers," Patterson said.

"No, he wasn't. He was up to something else entirely, although I'm sure the girl he had on his office desk probably got a passing grade considering what she was letting him do to her."

"Oh." Patterson's cheeks flushed red.

"I'm so sorry," Grant said.

"Me too." There was a hard edge to Linda's voice. "I spoke to a lawyer the next day and filed divorce papers. I also told Jeremy to be careful because the college had a strict policy about dating students. He didn't listen to me, even though the affair had already ruined our marriage. The college got wind of it, and that was that."

"What's he been doing since?" Grant asked. "Other than putting on his play?"

"Nothing, as far as I know. He moved out of the house and got himself an apartment, so it's not like I've seen him much over the last few months. But from what I heard, he seemed to think the play was his big break. A way to get back into professional theater. He even said being fired was the best thing that could have happened. Forced him to reevaluate his life. Goodness knows how he could afford to put a play on."

"Money was tight, then?" Patterson asked.

"It was for him after he lost his job. He wanted to take money from our joint savings account to fund the play, and I said no. I told him, when the divorce was finalized, he could do what he wanted with his share, but until then, the money was staying right where it was. Necessary expenses only for both of us. My lawyer made sure of that."

"So how did he fund the play?" Grant asked. "It can't be cheap, renting a theater and hiring actors."

"I suppose not. But I couldn't guess where he got the funds. Probably doing something shady. I asked him about it at our last meeting with the lawyers, but he refused to answer my questions. Just told me that the play was nothing to do with the divorce and I should keep my nose out. He had touched none of our bank accounts and nothing was unaccounted for, so there was little I could do. I asked my lawyer to look into it though, just to make sure he wasn't cheating me."

"And they didn't find anything?"

"No." Linda glanced up at the clock on the wall. "I'm afraid I'll have to end our conversation now. I have an appointment."

"Of course," Grant said. "Thank you for your time."

"If we have any more questions, we'll be in touch," Patterson said.

"Feel free. Call ahead and the front desk will let you know if I'm in the office." Linda stood up and gathered her purse, then she looked at the two FBI agents. "I hope you catch the animal who did this. Jeremy was a creep, and I wanted him to suffer for what he did, but he didn't deserve to die like that."

FOURTEEN

IT WAS three in the afternoon by the time they left Linda Knight's realty office. The gray clouds that had threatened rain for much of the day had thinned, and weak rays of sunshine struggled through. Patterson slipped her coat off and carried it over her shoulder.

Back in the car, she turned to Grant. "I guess we have our first real suspect."

"Those closest to the deceased are always high on the suspect list until we can rule them out," Grant replied. "And a messy divorce caused by a cheating husband does provide plenty of motive for an aggrieved wife. I'd like to do some digging on Linda Knight."

"What about her theory that an angry father did this?" Patterson asked. "It sounds like our victim was dipping his hand into pots he shouldn't have been."

"Agreed. A jealous boyfriend is also a possibility, and we should keep that in mind as we go forward."

"What's our next move?" Patterson asked.

"I think another visit to the crime scene is in order. Mrs. Knight posed some interesting questions, not the least of which is how the victim could afford to stage his play under the circumstances."

"We're going back to the theater?"

"I think it would be prudent. With any luck, Detective Ahlstrom will not be there." Grant turned the car on and eased out of their parking spot. "But first, I want to get some lunch. I saw a sandwich shop downtown. You in the mood for a spukie?"

"Sure. I could eat," Patterson grinned. "And what the hell is a spukie?"

"It's what we call sub sandwiches where I'm from. It's derived from the Italian word spucadella, which means long roll."

"You grew up in Italy?" Patterson shot Grant a quizzical look. "You don't look very Italian."

"I'm not. I grew up in the North End of Boston. There were a lot of Italian immigrants there."

"You're in New York now. Either call it a hero or go home."

"I'm sticking with spukie," Grant said as they pulled up outside the sandwich shop. "And I'm also hungry, so as your superior, I'm pulling rank and declaring this conversation over."

Thirty minutes later, their stomachs full, Grant and Patterson walked a block from the sandwich shop to the Phoenix Theater, where a rehearsal should have been underway for the murder victim's play. Instead, they found the front doors locked and the lobby dark. Someone had taped a sign to one of the doors announcing the theater was temporarily closed. Two police cars and a forensics van were parked outside.

Grant led Patterson around the side of the building and into the alley leading to the stage door. This was unlocked. They let themselves in and immediately bumped into a uniformed officer blocking their path. He was young, barely out of his teens, and looked bored. When he saw them enter, his demeanor changed.

"I can't let you folks in, I'm afraid," the cop said. "This is an active crime scene."

"We know that already." Grant flashed his credentials. "Special Agents Grant and Blake. FBI."

"Sorry. Didn't realize." The cop looked sheepish. He stepped aside to let them proceed. "If you're looking for Detective Ahlstrom, he's in the orchestra pit with forensics."

"We're not," Grant replied. "We'd like to talk to a member of the theater staff. Someone familiar with the play. I don't suppose anyone is here?"

"Most of the staff were given the day off. The artistic director is here, though. Said she had work to do and promised to stay out of the way."

"And where can we find her?" Patterson asked.

The cop glanced around toward a door marked *Private. Staff Only*. "She's in her office, through there."

"Thank you." Grant sidestepped the policeman and

made his way to the door, beyond which was a short corridor with offices on both sides. Only one was occupied.

The Phoenix Theater's artistic director was a plump woman in her fifties, with graying hair and a droopy face. She looked up as they approached. "May I help you?"

"Yes, ma'am. I hope so." Grant introduced himself and Patterson, then got right to the point. "We're hoping you can give us some information about the play that should've been running here. Specifically, about the theater company staging it and Jeremy Knight."

"That poor man," the woman said. "I can't believe he was killed right here in our theater. And in such a violent way. It gives me the creeps every time I think about it, to be honest. I'm not sure anyone will feel safe until you catch the murderer."

"That's our plan, miss…?"

"Gloria Gleason."

"Thank you, Miss Gleason. What can you tell me about Jeremy Knight?"

"His theater company is called Knight Players. This was going to be their first production, I believe. Mr. Knight had been out of the business for a while, teaching until he lost his job. The play was going to be his way back into theater."

"Yes, we know that already," Patterson said. "We're more interested in how he was able to put together the funds to stage a play. Were you giving him a discounted rate for the theater?"

"Yes," Gloria replied. "Things won't really get going around here until later in June. That's when the tourist season kicks in, and the beaches fill up. We can't charge premium rates during the off-season because there aren't as many people to buy tickets. As it is, the play was barely selling."

"Did he pay a deposit?"

Gloria nodded. "Thirty percent down and the rest on opening night."

"How did he pay that?" Grant asked.

"He wrote a check."

"I don't suppose you still have it?"

"Sure. We make all of our deposits electronically now. It's just easier." Gloria went to the filing cabinet and rummaged through it, then turned back to them with a manila file in her hand. She opened it and found the check, then handed it to Grant. "Here you are."

Grant studied the check for a moment, then passed it over to Patterson. "Fifteen hundred bucks drawn on a business account. Knight Players, LLC."

"Interesting," Patterson said. "Mrs. Knight told us she refused Jeremy's request for money from their joint bank account."

Grant nodded and took a photograph of the check with his phone before handing it back to Gloria. "I don't suppose you know how the theater company was funded?"

"Sorry. No." Gloria bit her bottom lip. "I wish I could be more helpful."

"I assume you were selling tickets through your box office. What happens to the money from those?"

"We hold it until after the performance, and then it gets deposited into the theater company bank account. Minus credit card fees and other expenses, of course."

"That means Jeremy Knight wouldn't have access to those funds until the week of the show."

"Correct," Gloria said. "Not that it mattered much. As I said, they'd barely sold any tickets. To be honest, we were a little worried he might not pay us the balance owed for the theater rental. Unless there was a significant uptick in sales, the play was going to lose a lot of money."

Grant nodded slowly. "Thank you, Miss Gleason, you've been very helpful."

"My pleasure. Please come back if you think of anything else."

"We will," Grant replied before turning to leave.

Back out on the street, he stopped and turned to Patterson. "What do you make of it all?"

Patterson thought for a moment before speaking. "The theater company was obviously struggling, and Jeremy Knight didn't have access to funds from ticket sales yet."

"And we know he didn't get money from his wife."

"Which means he found it some other way." Patterson glanced down the street. "You want to visit the bank? Maybe they can tell us where the money came from."

"No. They won't tell us anything without a subpoena, and it will take a while to get that. Right now, I think we head back to the hotel and see what we can find out about the theater company's LLC. There's something not quite right about all of this, and I want to know what."

FIFTEEN

AT SEVEN-THIRTY THAT EVENING, Grant knocked on Patterson's hotel room door and suggested they get dinner. They had spent the afternoon working separately, with Grant researching the theater company and Patterson looking into the wife.

They drove a couple of miles down the road to a hole-in-the-wall pizza joint and ordered a large pepperoni to split before sharing the afternoon's discoveries.

"I looked up the theater company's LLC filing," Grant said as they waited for the food to arrive. "The company was established a month ago with Jeremy Knight as the sole owner. Looks like he filed the paperwork himself. Other than an address for the apartment he rented after moving out of the family home, there isn't much more information there."

"It tells us he didn't go into business with someone else," Patterson said. "Nixing the possibility that he was the creative talent while a partner provided the funds."

"Right. Doesn't rule out there being an investor, but they don't own a share of the theater company."

"You really think someone would drop their hard-earned cash into an unproven theater company that's struggling to sell tickets for its first and only production?"

"That's a question we need to answer," Grant said, thoughtfully. "I also contacted Linda Knight's divorce lawyer. He knows nothing about the theater company bank account, and it wasn't mentioned in any of the financial paperwork submitted by Jeremy."

"He was hiding assets?"

"Not necessarily. They were already separated when he set up the business, so he wasn't obliged to include the LLC unless it was funded by joint money."

"Which we know it wasn't."

"Correct."

"None of which gets us any closer to figuring out where he got the cash to stage his play. We know he wasn't working because the college had fired him at that point." Patterson furrowed her brow. "Unless he took another job somewhere else."

"If he did, Linda Knight wasn't aware of it. Plus, I got a copy of the rehearsal schedule for the play, and he's been at the theater every day for the last two weeks. If he did have another job, it must have been part-time and certainly wouldn't have provided enough money for the theater company's needs." When the pizza arrived, Grant fell silent. He waited for the waiter to leave before continuing. "Did you find out anything useful this afternoon?"

"You could say that." Patterson deposited a slice of pie

onto her plate. "I think I might have gotten us another suspect."

"Really?" Grant's eyebrows shot up. "Who?"

"Linda Knight has a brother. A guy named Stephen Canning. He's a mechanic. Works for a place over in East Hampton. And get this, he has a record for assault."

"Interesting." Grant dug into his pizza and started to eat. "What's his deal?"

"He got into a bar fight about ten years ago. Punched a guy who was chatting to his girlfriend."

"A drunken brawl over a girl doesn't make him a murderer."

"I agree. But that isn't the only incident. Six years ago, he was living in Queens and working for an auto body repair place. There was an altercation with a disgruntled customer. Words were exchanged. He went after the guy with a ball peen hammer."

"Now we're talking," Grant said. He sat forward and rested his elbows on the table. "What happened?"

"No one actually got hurt. Couple of the other employees broke it up in the nick of time. The customer filed a police report and Canning was arrested. He got a suspended sentence after pleading to a lesser charge. Cost him his job, too. The auto body place wanted nothing to do with him."

"Which is understandable. Employees going after customers with a hammer can't be good for business."

"But it shows a proclivity for violence and the hammer is his weapon of choice."

"And I'm sure he doesn't like Jeremy Knight very much,

given what the guy did to his sister. Might have wanted to teach our victim a lesson."

"Makes sense. He'd certainly have the strength to commit such a crime," Grant said. "You have the address for his current employer?"

"Yes. It's in my phone already."

"Good." Grant settled back in his chair. "Let's pay Stephen Canning a visit first thing in the morning. See what he has to say for himself."

"Sounds good to me." Patterson polished off a second slice of pizza. She looked at the remaining pizza on a tray stand next to the table. "You want any more of this?"

"Nah. I've had a couple of slices already. I think I'm good," Grant said with a grin. He patted his belly. "Gotta watch my figure."

"Didn't bother you earlier when you were demolishing that footlong hero."

"That's because it wasn't swimming in grease. And I told you already, it's a spukie."

"Right. How could I forget." Patterson looked at the pizza. "Last chance."

"Really. I'm good." Grant shook his head.

"Well, in that case," Patterson said, glancing around for their server to ask for a to-go box, "we'll take it back to the hotel. I love cold pizza for breakfast."

SIXTEEN

AFTER DINNER, they returned to the hotel. Grant escorted Patterson to her room and stepped inside while she forwarded him the information she had uncovered on Stephen Canning.

When it was done, she looked up from her laptop. "There. You should have it in your email any moment now."

Grant thanked her and held out the pizza box. He glanced toward the mini-fridge sitting under the counter next to the hotel room's sink. "Got room for this in there?"

"Keep it. You might get hungry. You only had a couple of slices."

"Honestly, I don't need the temptation. I try to avoid eating right before bed. You probably have more willpower than me." Grant went to the fridge and slid the pizza box in. When he turned back, his gaze roamed to the nightstand, and the silver frame sitting upon it. He walked over and picked it up. "What's this?"

"Memories of the past," Patterson said. "My dad gave it to me last night before you called and spirited me here."

"One of these two girls you?" Grant looked up from studying the photo inside the frame.

Patterson nodded. "Me and my sister."

"It's hard to tell which one you are," Grant said. "You both look so alike."

"Not so much. My hair was lighter, and our eyes aren't the same color. Mine are blue."

"And your sister?"

"Gray, which is quite rare, apparently."

Grant studied the photo. "Still doesn't help me."

"I'm on the left. The younger one who doesn't look like she'd rather be shopping."

"Ah. Sister doesn't like fishing, huh?"

"Didn't. Past tense." Patterson stood and crossed the room. She took the frame from Grant's hand and placed it back on the nightstand.

Grant stepped away, looking sheepish. "I have a feeling I just put my foot in my mouth."

Patterson shook her head. "It's personal, that's all."

"Well, I apologize anyway. I didn't mean to overstep my bounds."

"Don't worry about it." Patterson sat on the edge of the bed and looked at the photograph, then up at Grant. "But you must know about my sister already. Surely you've seen my Bureau file."

"Why? Because I have your home address? I told you, I make it a point to know where all my agents live so I can mobilize them at a moment's notice. That doesn't mean I went down to admin and stalked you. Besides, I couldn't even if I wanted to. I'm a Supervisory Special Agent, not your SAC. They won't let me go wandering around the personnel files willy-nilly."

"I just assumed you knew."

"You could tell me now."

"It really isn't that interesting."

"Whatever happened clearly affected you, judging by your reaction." Grant sat on the bed next to her. "Look, you don't have to talk about it, but if you ever want to unburden, I'll listen."

"I appreciate that." Patterson looked at her watch. "It's still early. I saw a bar not far from the hotel when we were driving back. We can walk there. Want to grab a drink?"

"I don't think so. It might be better if we got an early night." Grant stood up. "I don't want to hang around in the morning. If Stephen Canning is our man, I'd like to know that sooner rather than later."

"Of course." Patterson watched Grant make his way to the hotel room door. Before he stepped out, she spoke again. "My sister's name was Julie. She was six years older than me."

Grant stopped and turned back to her. He stood wordlessly in the doorway, his soft eyes searching her face.

"She went off to college not long after that photo was taken. Then she disappeared."

Grant swallowed. "I'm sorry to hear that."

"Me too." Patterson felt a tear weave its way down her cheek. She met Grant's gaze.

When it became apparent she wasn't going to elaborate

further, Grant cleared his throat. "Sleep tight, Special Agent Blake. Sleep tight." With that, he swiveled and walked through the door, closing it behind him.

Patterson sat on the bed for a while, lost in thoughts of her sister, then she rose and got ready for bed. She wasn't sure why she'd told Jonathan Grant about Julie. She rarely opened up about the trauma of her teenage years and her sister's disappearance. It was a family matter. Private. But there was something about the handsome special agent. Despite his rugged exterior, he possessed a gentle nature that made her feel safe. And even though he was at least eight years her senior, she couldn't help feeling an attraction to him. Maybe it was because she hadn't made time for romantic relationships since being selected for Quantico, and now she was thrust into close quarters with this self-assured and capable man who wasn't exactly hard to look at. Or maybe she was just lonely and wanted more out of life than an empty apartment and dinner once a week with her father.

Either way, it didn't matter. She could hardly act on her feelings. They were coworkers. Actually, not even that. He was her superior and the Bureau surely had some kind of rule about fraternizing. Besides, when he looked at her, Jonathan Grant probably just saw a rookie agent still wet behind the ears. Deciding that her sudden and surprising attraction to Special Agent Jonathan Grant was nothing more than a momentary infatuation at best, and a terrible idea at worst, Patterson pushed all thoughts of the man from her mind, switched on the TV, and climbed into bed.

Twenty minutes later, her phone buzzed. She picked it up to find a text message from Grant.

Thank you for sharing with me about Julie.
I know how hard it must have been for you.

Patterson read the message, her fingers hovering over the screen as she contemplated a reply, but then she placed the phone back on the nightstand without answering. Jonathan Grant had gotten under her skin tonight, and Patterson wasn't sure how she felt about that.

SEVENTEEN

GRANT ARRIVED at Patterson's door early the next morning carrying two large cups of coffee for the second day in a row.

"You want to be careful about that," she said, nodding toward the coffee cups as she let him inside. "I'll get used to this, and you'll be stuck bringing me coffee every morning."

"I've had worse jobs," Grant replied with a smile. "You ready to hit the road, partner?"

"Sure." Patterson had been up and dressed for half an hour already. In the cold light of day, her sudden attraction to Grant the night before felt foolish, but even so, her stomach betrayed her with a little flip when she looked at him. Ignoring it, she slipped her Glock into its shoulder holster and pulled on a jacket to cover the weapon. "We off to see Stephen Canning?"

"That's the plan." Grant turned back toward the door.

"Hang on." Patterson ran to the fridge and opened it. She pulled out the pizza box and then hurried after Grant.

He shot her a quizzical look as she closed the hotel room door and followed him down the sidewalk toward the car. "You're really doing that?"

"What?"

"Pizza for breakfast."

"Damn right." Patterson nodded. "Nothing better to get the day started."

"I'll take your word for that." Grant unlocked the car.

"Want some?" Patterson asked, climbing into the passenger side and opening the box.

"I think I'll pass."

"Your loss." Patterson plucked a large slice out, peeling hardened cheese from the bottom of the box along with it, and took a bite. "This is really good. If anything, it's better than last night."

"Again..."

"I know. You'll take my word for it." She munched happily on the pizza as they drove through town and picked up State Route Twenty-Seven west toward East Hampton. Fifteen minutes later, they arrived at an industrial park full of small warehouses with roll-up bay doors. An assortment of transit vans and medium-sized trucks were pulled up to the units, some being loaded with goods, while others were parked.

The auto repair shop that employed Stephen Canning was at the end of a row next to a grassy area filled with cars, some of which looked like they hadn't moved in a long time.

The bay door was up, and they could see an SUV sitting on a lift inside with a mechanic working underneath it.

Grant pulled up behind a Chevy Impala with a crushed front bumper. "This must be the place."

Patterson watched the man working under the car. "I wonder if that's him?"

"Only one way to find out." Grant unbuckled his seatbelt, opened his door, and stepped out of the car.

Patterson did the same, and together they walked toward the repair shop.

When they entered, the mechanic looked around. "Can I help you?"

"We're looking for Stephen Canning. Is that you?"

"Who wants to know?"

"FBI," Grant replied, flashing his credentials. "Are you Stephen Canning?"

"No." The mechanic looked nervous. He clearly wasn't used to federal agents showing up at his work. He turned and shouted to another mechanic further back in the building. "Hey, Frankie. Where's Steve?"

"Out back I think. Said he was going for a smoke."

The mechanic turned back to Patterson and Grant. "He's out by the back door."

"How do we get there?" Grant asked.

The mechanic nodded toward a corridor behind an office with a large glass window overlooking the bays. "Go down there past the restrooms and turn left. Last door."

"Thanks." Grant took off, following the mechanic's directions.

Patterson followed behind. "It's a bit early for a break, don't you think?"

"I guess he's not a model employee," Grant said as they approached the door, which was propped open with a brick to stop it from closing all the way.

Stephen Canning was standing on the other side, leaning against the building's back wall, sucking on a cigarette. When they stepped outside, he straightened up and pursed his lips to release a stream of smoke.

"You two must be lost. This is a private area. Employees only."

"We're not lost," Grant said, not bothering to confirm the man's identity thanks to a name tag stitched onto his blue overalls. "We're here to see you."

"Me?" Canning flicked the remains of the cigarette onto the ground and crushed it with his heel. "Mind telling me who you are?"

Grant handled the introductions, noting how Canning's face drained of color when he realized they were federal agents. "We'd like to ask you a few questions about your sister and her husband."

"Her husband's dead. Someone had the good sense to see him off with a hammer."

"We know that." Patterson didn't bother to hide the contempt in her voice. "You don't seem very upset about it."

"Why should I be? The man was a scumbag. He was running around on Linda."

"We know that, too," Grant said. "What we don't know is who killed him."

"Let me guess, you saw my past transgressions and thought I had something to do with it."

"It crossed our minds."

"Well, I didn't." Canning dug his hands into his pockets. "I haven't seen Jeremy Knight for months. Not since my sister kicked him out."

"You sure about that?" Patterson asked.

"I think I'd know if I'd seen him."

"You have an alibi for the night of the murder?" Grant stepped closer to Canning as if he expected him to run.

The man didn't run. Instead, he met Grant's gaze with cool indifference. "Not that you could verify."

"That's convenient," Patterson said.

"I wasn't expecting to need one or I wouldn't have been so careless."

"Okay, we get the point," Grant said. "Tell us where you were, anyway."

"I was at home all night. Watched a movie then went to bed before midnight."

"Alone?"

Canning nodded. "I'm between girlfriends right now."

"And you never left the house all evening?"

"Not until I left for work the next morning." Canning glanced toward the door. "If you don't have any more questions, I have a busted radiator to fix."

"I think we're done for now," Grant said.

"Thank you." Canning pushed past the two FBI agents and went to step back into the building.

Grant stepped aside to let him pass, then spoke again. "What movie?"

"Huh?" Canning turned back to them, confused.

"What movie did you watch?"

"I don't see how that's relevant."

"I'm curious, is all."

"The flick about the killer shark. Jaws. It was on one of those classic movie channels. We good now?"

Grant nodded.

Canning lingered for a moment, looking at the agents, then he turned and disappeared back into the building.

EIGHTEEN

"YOU BELIEVE Linda Knight's brother when he said he hasn't seen her husband for months?" Patterson asked as they drove back toward Montauk from East Hampton.

"I have no reason to disbelieve him," Grant answered. "But that doesn't mean he's telling the truth."

"Is that why you asked him about the movie?"

"I figured it was worth seeing if he at least had an answer."

Patterson was tapping on her phone. After a moment, she let out an exclamation. "And it was the correct one. Jaws was playing two nights ago on TCM. Came on at 10 o'clock."

"Just because he knew the movie was on doesn't mean he watched it. Not that we have any way of finding out one way or the other."

"So where does that leave us?"

"Still on the hunt for answers, just like before." Grant paused, thoughtful. "There are several restaurants near the theater. I wonder if anyone saw anything unusual the night of the killing."

"I'm sure Detective Ahlstrom has already taken statements."

"As we've already established, I prefer to ask my own questions. I think it's time we knock on some doors. The customers will be long gone, but some of the staff might have been working that night. Maybe we'll get lucky and find a witness that can blow this thing open."

"It's worth a try. We don't have any other leads," Patterson said. "Might be worth paying a visit to Jeremy Knight's apartment, too."

"Great minds think alike. It was already on my to-do list for today. I cleared it with Detective Ahlstrom this morning while I was picking up the coffee. He's making arrangements for us to go there later today."

"The guy must love you, with all these early morning calls," Patterson said as they entered Montauk's Main Street and found a place to park.

"He wasn't exactly friendly." Grant turned the engine off and opened his door. "I have to confess, I called him early on purpose. The man's attitude rankles me. He had no right to treat you so badly when we arrived at the murder scene."

"It's fine. Not the first time I've encountered an attitude like that, and I'm sure it won't be the last."

"Doesn't make it okay." Grant climbed out of the car and waited for Patterson to join him. He looked left and right, summing up their best targets, then nodded toward an Italian restaurant down the block with a dining area set up on the sidewalk. "That seems like a good place to start."

"I doubt anyone was eating outside," Patterson said as they started toward the trattoria. "They must've been just about closing up when the murder took place, not to mention how chilly it was that night."

"Still worth a shot. With any luck, one of the staff members saw something when they were leaving work."

Patterson was about to say that if they did, Detective Ahlstrom had probably already spoken to them and knew about it, when she stopped in her tracks. Something had drawn her eyes toward the storefront they were now passing. It was a clothing shop, the window full of gaudy cruise wear. But it wasn't the brightly colored shirts and hideously patterned dresses that had caught her attention. It was a much smaller item attached to the ceiling in the top corner of the window. Angled to face the store's front door, it would also catch a wide swath of the street outside.

A compact security camera tucked almost out of sight.

Patterson grabbed at Grant's arm. "I bet the angle of that camera is wide enough for us to see the front of the theater."

"I think you're right," Grant said, his voice rising with excitement.

"And what's more, I'll also bet Detective Ahlstrom completely missed it. I only saw it because I happened to glance up at exactly the right time. It's barely noticeable up in the corner like that."

"And this is why we check everything ourselves." Grant was already moving toward the door. "This investigation is turning out to be excellent field training."

"Bet you're glad you brought me along," Patterson said, pleased with herself. "Even you walked right past it."

"Don't get cocky." Grant pushed the door open and stepped into the store. Above them, a bell jangled to alert the store clerk that they had customers. "No one likes a gloater."

"I'm not gloating," Patterson said, indignant. "I was just pointing out—"

"Well, what do we have here?" A middle-aged woman with bleach blond hair appeared, interrupting Patterson mid-sentence. "A couple of lovebirds off on a cruise, looking for matching outfits?"

"Oh, we're not together," Patterson said quickly.

"And we're not going on a cruise," Grant added, his voice a low rumble. "I can't stand cruises."

"Well, now, that's a shame. You make such a cute couple. You look…" The woman paused, summing them up. "Right for each other."

"Do we?" The words tripped from Patterson's mouth before she realized what she was saying. Her cheeks flushed.

Grant rolled his eyes and pointed toward the security camera. "Does that thing work?"

"Why, yes. We put it in last year. We've had some problems with shoplifters."

"Really?" Grant said, his eyes roaming the mannequins decked out in fluorescent jackets, neon sundresses, and Hawaiian shirts.

"Given your interest in the camera, I assume you aren't here to shop," the woman said, sounding a little disappointed.

"That's correct," Patterson replied, identifying herself and Grant as FBI agents before getting to the point. "We're investigating the murder two nights ago at the Phoenix Theater."

"I heard about that. A nasty business." The woman's voice had lost its joviality. "Such a shame. We were providing costumes for the play in exchange for an advertisement in the program. I guess that won't be happening now."

"I really couldn't say," Grant said. "Does the camera work twenty-four hours a day?"

"Yes." The woman glanced toward the camera. "It's wired up to a laptop in my office. Records onto the hard drive. We keep the recordings for thirty days as standard, then delete them."

"So you have footage from the time the murder took place?"

"Why yes, I suppose we might. I hadn't thought of that. Otherwise, I would've taken a look and contacted the police. The camera has an excellent field of view. You can see the street all the way down to the theater."

"Would you mind if we see it?" Patterson asked.

"Sure. Come this way." The woman turned and headed toward the back of the store. She led them into an office with racks of metal shelving on one side stacked high with boxes marked *made in China*. On the other side was a desk with the aforementioned laptop sitting upon it. An older Windows machine with a large screen.

The woman sat at the desk and pecked at the keyboard, browsing through folders until she found one marked with the date of the murder. Inside were dozens of video files saved with timestamps. She looked up at the FBI agents. "The camera doesn't record continuously. That would fill the hard drive up. It's activated by motion. It often picks up cars and trucks driving down the street. Not so much at that time of night, though. There's not a lot of traffic around after the stores close."

"What about pedestrians on the sidewalk?" Patterson asked.

"It picks them up if they're close to the camera," the woman answered. "It will have recorded the two of you coming into the store. But all the way down by the theater, it's unlikely a pedestrian would activate it, especially in the dark. We don't have the sensitivity set high because the camera would be going off every five seconds during the day. We're really only interested in recording folk who come into the store."

Patterson looked at Grant. "If our killer was on foot, this camera will be useless."

"I'd still like to see what we've got," Grant said.

"Here we go," the woman said. "There's only a handful of files from late that night, at least until the cops showed up."

Patterson and Grant edged closer to the desk, leaning over her shoulder as the woman opened the video files one by one. Mostly, they showed cars driving past and continuing on their way. One recording was different, however. It captured a pickup truck pulling up outside. The driver's door opened, and a figure got out, barely visible in the darkness. A figure that disappeared into the alley where the stage door was located. A couple of minutes later, the figure reappeared, running this time, and jumped back into the truck before speeding off.

"I guess we got lucky," Grant said. "Our killer was good enough to trip the camera with his truck."

"Question is, who was it?" Patterson asked. "It's so dark he's nothing but a blurry shape."

"The driver might not be recognizable, but we may be able to read the number plate on his truck," Grant said. He addressed the store clerk. "Can you make this any bigger?"

"I can, but it'll be hard to see," she replied. "It's a cheap camera, and there's no night vision."

"I'll take what I can get." Grant pointed at the truck's rear. "Zoom in on that license plate."

The clerk obliged, tapping a small plus symbol at the bottom right corner of the video app until the license plate filled the viewing area.

"It's hard to make out," Patterson said, disappointed. "I can only read the last three digits. Three One Zero. The rest is in shadow."

"It's better than nothing." Grant took out his phone and snapped a picture of the screen. He tapped the clerk on the shoulder. "If I give you my email address, can you send me that video file?"

"Sure." The woman shrugged.

"Great." Grant turned to Patterson. "I'll send this over to the office right away. Get them working on it."

"There can't be that many pickup trucks registered with those three last digits," Patterson said.

"I agree," Grant replied. "And once we find out who owns that truck, odds are we've got our killer."

NINETEEN

THEY SPENT the next ninety minutes going door to door along both sides of Main Street, visiting all the businesses that might have been open after rehearsal ended the night of the murder, but no one had seen anything. The surveillance camera footage was their only clue and even though they uncovered no more leads, Grant had high hopes that the partial license plate would lead them to Jeremy Knight's killer. Now they were back in the car and heading away from the center of town. As they drove, he called Ahlstrom and conversed briefly with him.

"We can head straight over to Knight's apartment," Grant said, hanging up. "The detective has tracked down the building manager and arranged for him to meet us there with a passkey. He's sent one of his own men too, under the guise of inter-agency cooperation."

"That's very magnanimous of him."

"I don't think he likes us, but the man isn't stupid. He

needs our help, and he knows it." Grant turned onto a side road and followed it until they came to Knight's apartment building, a three-story Victorian with a wraparound porch, bright white siding, and dark blue shutters. A tall oak tree stood in the yard, blocking most of the sunlight. An area to the left of the building that must once have been a garden was now paved over to provide parking for the tenants. There were only three vehicles in the lot, one of which was an unmarked Crown Victoria that obviously belonged to the man in a crumpled suit standing outside near the porch.

"That must be the detective Ahlstrom sent to meet us," Grant said, pulling into a bay next to the unmarked police car.

"Let's go say hello," Patterson said, opening her car door.

Together, they crossed the parking lot and walked up the path toward the porch.

As they approached, the detective moved to greet them, extending a hand. "You must be the FBI agents. I'm Detective Jim Layton."

Grant nodded and introduced himself and Patterson, shaking the man's hand, then glanced around. "Nice place. This must've been a big house before it was converted into rental units."

"Historic building," Layton replied. "Belonged to some senator or other back in the day. Shame they broke it up into apartments, but I guess it's easier to rent that way. Knight's apartment is on the second floor. The building manager is waiting up there with the keys."

"Lead the way," Grant said as the detective turned and stepped up onto the porch.

They made their way inside and through a wide lobby with a tile floor, then up a set of stairs to the second floor. There were three apartments on this level. The building manager, a squat man with thinning gray hair and a bulging waistline, was waiting near the furthest door at the end of a short and dimly lit hallway.

"This is Mr. Garrett," the detective said. "He's kindly agreed to let us into the apartment."

"Beats dealing with the blocked sewage pipe that was on my schedule before you guys called," Garrett said. "I was mighty sad to hear about Mr. Knight. I only met him once, but he seemed nice. Hope you get the scum who killed him and lock them away for a long time."

"That's why we're here," Grant said, motioning toward the door. "Would you mind?"

"Oh, sure." Garrett unclipped a ring packed with keys from his belt. He sorted through them until he came to the correct one, then unlocked the door. He pushed it open and stood aside. "All yours."

"Thanks." Grant, Patterson, and Layton entered the apartment. When Garrett moved to follow, he turned and stopped the building manager. "I'd rather you wait out in the hallway if you don't mind."

"Right. Of course." Garrett nodded, looking a little disappointed. "Tell you what. I've got some work to do down in the basement. Hot water heater on the fritz. Why don't you come and get me when you're finished."

"Sounds good," Grant said. He watched the building manager retreat down the hallway and then turned his attention back to the apartment.

"Anything in particular you're looking for?" Layton asked. "We already went over this place yesterday. Didn't find anything worth a damn."

"We'll see," Grant said, walking past the detective into the apartment's living room. He turned to Patterson and nodded toward an open door. "Why don't you take the bedroom and I'll search out here."

"You need me for anything?" The detective asked.

"I think we're good," Grant told him.

"In that case, I'll be out on the front porch. I got some calls to make, anyway." The detective turned and left.

Patterson heard his footsteps recede down the hallway and then on the stairs. As Grant started searching the living room, she made her way to the bedroom and looked around.

There was a queen bed against the far wall beneath a simple brass headboard. A crumpled linen duvet and a pair of pillows covered it. Atop a low cabinet was an assortment of books, mostly nonfiction titles on scriptwriting and directing. A cheap-looking desk sat under the window with an equally inexpensive office chair pushed under it. There was an older model notebook computer on top with the screen open. Deciding that was the most likely place to find something of relevance, Patterson went straight to the desk. She removed a pair of latex gloves from her pocket and pulled them on, before nudging the chair aside.

At first, Patterson saw nothing of interest. Just the laptop computer and a dirty coffee mug. But inside the desk drawer, she found a stack of paperwork, mostly from the divorce lawyer. There was a list of assets, which Patterson noted did not include the theater company or its associated bank account. There were several court documents, mortgage statements, and tax returns. Then, at the bottom of the pile, Patterson found pay dirt. She snatched the paperwork up, skimmed through it, and then called to Grant.

He appeared in the bedroom doorway a moment later, eyes wide with expectation. "What have you got?"

"A legal contract relating to the theater company." Patterson showed him the paperwork. "An agreement between Jeremy Knight and a company that goes by the name of Candlewood Investments. Looks like this is where he got the money to fund the theater company."

"Did you say Candlewood Investments?"

"You know it?"

"Yeah. I know it. How much did they give Knight?"

"Thirty-five thousand."

Grant whistled. "That's a lot of dough to invest in a struggling theater company with no proven track record."

"I agree," Patterson said. "I think we should find out who owns Candlewood Investments and go have a chat with them."

"No need. I know exactly where to find the man behind Candlewood Investments." Grant was already on his way out of the apartment. "Come on. And bring that paperwork with you."

"Where are we going?"

"To get answers," Grant said as he hurried down the stairs toward the front door. "I have a good feeling about this. A very good feeling."

TWENTY

"WHERE ARE WE GOING?" Patterson asked as they drove away from Jeremy Knight's apartment building toward the western shore of Lake Montauk. "And how come you know about Candlewood Investments?"

"Bruce Russo." Grant kept his eyes on the road but spoke through gritted teeth. "He's been on the FBI's radar for a couple of decades because of his financial dealings and the fact that he's a suspected mobster. I worked on a task force targeting him back when I was a junior agent. But we could make nothing stick."

"He's the man behind Candlewood Investments, I assume," Patterson said.

"It's one of many companies he owns. He operates it mostly as a shell corporation to funnel funds from his illicit activities to legitimize the profits."

"You're talking about money laundering."

"And the theater company is a great place to do that."

"Still, thirty-five grand is a lot of cash to give Jeremy Knight for a show with barely any ticket sales. I find it hard to believe he'd get enough of his investment back to make it worthwhile."

"I agree. Which is why I want to have a chat with him."

"Now all we have to do is find him."

"It won't be that hard. I've kept my hand in with the task force since moving on and up in the Bureau. Russo fancies himself as a land developer. Another good way to launder money. He's building a high-end hotel and yacht club out on Westlake Drive near Star Island. He bought the land years ago and just got around to developing it. Word is, it's his new pet project. If he's anywhere, he'll be there."

"And if he's not?"

"Then I'll call up my buddy on the task force. He'll know where Russo is."

"How long has this task force been running?"

"Almost twelve years. Truth is, it's really more of a one-man operation at this point. CID decided there were bigger fish to fry. Russo wasn't high enough up the food chain to warrant the resources, apparently. Still, they can't quite let go, so they kept an agent on him."

Patterson nodded. CID was the Criminal Investigative Division of the FBI, tasked with investigating mail fraud and racketeering, among other things. "You think he's involved in Jeremy Knight's death?"

"I don't know what to think," Grant admitted. "Linda Knight's brother, Stephen Canning, has a record of violence and a motive. He also doesn't have a solid alibi for the night of the murder."

"But as Canning pointed out, he wasn't aware he would need one. If he was intending to commit murder, surely he would have prepared a little better."

"Not if it was a crime of passion. Maybe he lost his temper. Still, the connection to Bruce Russo is intriguing." Grant slowed the car. They were approaching a construction site surrounded by chain-link fencing on the right-hand side. An imposing multi story building was being erected near the water. Beyond this was a marina with empty boat slips. But it was the structure under construction standing apart from the main building that caught Patterson's eye. A full-size replica of a lighthouse, complete with a keeper's cottage. The tower looked like it had been there for decades, but the construction materials and scaffolding surrounding it told a different story.

The construction site was open, the gates open. As they drove through, their car bumping off the smooth road to a graded but unfinished driveway, Patterson noticed a large sign standing near the entrance.

Coming Soon from
Russo Property Development.
Lighthouse Point.
Luxury Condo Hotel and Marina.

That explained the fake lighthouse. She peered up at the imposing structure as they drew closer and wondered how much it would cost to stay in such a place. More than she could afford, no doubt.

Grant brought the car to a stop near a cluster of portable

buildings sitting on muddy dirt that would probably be lush green lawns not too long from now. He climbed out and made for the nearest one, with the words Construction Foreman's Office stenciled on the door. He climbed the steps and disappeared inside.

Patterson followed along behind, but before she could enter the small cabin office, Grant reemerged.

"We're in luck. Russo is here," Grant said. "He's in the hotel lobby overseeing the installation of a seventeenth-century sculpture he had imported from Italy."

"Isn't that a little extravagant for Long Island?" Patterson asked.

"Don't ask me. This is my first time in a yacht club." Grant started toward the hotel, trudging across the dirt and weaving around construction materials sitting on pallets near the entrance.

The upscale hotel lobby was almost complete. A grand staircase sweeping two floors up provided a dramatic focal point. The floors were covered in polished marble. The walls were finished in dark wood paneling that make the place look as if it had been there for a century or more. Enormous windows at the far end of the lobby offered panoramic views of the marina and Lake Montauk beyond that. An enormous chandelier made with thousands of cut-glass pieces rested on a tarp in the center of the space, waiting to be installed. To their left, workmen bustled in what Patterson guessed would one day be a high-end restaurant. She could see the bar area at the back, still in pieces and waiting to be assembled.

The aforementioned Italian sculpture, a marble of two

female figures in a tight embrace with flowing robes twisting around them as if tugged by some unseen breeze, stood near the panoramic windows bathed in natural light. Three men in hardhats stood around the sculpture, deep in discussion. Two wore dirty jeans and shirts. The third, a neatly groomed older gentleman with a stocky frame and jet-black hair, was dressed in a fine suit. This, Patterson surmised, must be who they had come here to see.

He turned at their approach. "This is a closed construction site. Who are you?"

"Federal agents," Grant said, letting the man see his badge. "Bruce Russo?"

"That's me." Russo observed them with suspicious eyes. "If you're here to search the place, don't bother. Everything's nice and legal."

"We're here to talk with you," Grant replied.

"I'm busy." Russo turned back toward the statue. "Come back another time."

"I don't think so." Grant stood his ground and waited for Russo to turn back toward him. "We can either have our chat here, or we can go somewhere you will find less comfortable. Your choice."

"Should I be calling my lawyer?"

"Not so far as I know. Unless you're planning to confess a crime."

"You wish."

"Then you won't mind sparing a moment of your time."

"Fine." Russo sighed. "I have an office on the other side of the site. We can talk there."

TWENTY-ONE

BRUCE RUSSO LED the two FBI agents out of the lobby and across the construction site to a portable building standing aside from the others. A door marked PRIVATE–NO ADMITTANCE was the only thing that identified it as his office. He pulled a key from his pocket and unlocked the door, then ushered them inside.

The well-appointed interior surprised Patterson. She had expected a stark and utilitarian office but instead found herself in an office decorated so sumptuously it would not have been out of place in one of the gilded mansions on New York's Fifth Avenue. A fine Persian rug covered the floor. An oak desk filled one end of the room, behind which stood an ornate liquor cabinet flanked by two cherry bookcases filled with volumes. Wall sconces cast a soft yellow glow around the room, replacing the more standard fluorescent lighting that was normally found in such buildings. A small sitting area with a leather loveseat and two wingback chairs clustered around an antique coffee table filled out the space.

"Wow," Patterson said. "This isn't at all what I expected."

"I like to be comfortable," Russo said, standing near one of the leather chairs and motioning for Patterson and Grant to sit on the loveseat. "I would offer you both a drink, but I'm sure you would just refuse, being on duty and all."

"You are correct," Grant said.

"Well, I don't have to abide by any such rules." Russo went to the liquor cabinet and took out a cut crystal tumbler, into which he poured a large measure of neat scotch from an equally fancy decanter. He returned to the sitting area and settled into the closest chair, sipping the drink with obvious pleasure. "It's a shame you can't join me. You really are missing a treat. Thirty-year single malt matured in Sherry-seasoned casks. Delicious."

"We'll take your word for it," Grant said. "Can we begin?"

"Fire away." Russo leaned back in the chair and studied his whiskey. "What would you like to ask me?"

"We're here about Jeremy Knight and the Knight Players." Grant sat with his hands in his lap, eyes fixed upon Russo.

"I'm sorry, who?"

"Jeremy Knight. I assume you know him."

Russo shook his head slowly. "I don't think I've—"

"Before you go any further, I should warn you we know about the investment you made with his theater company."

"Investment? I don't think I've... what was the name of the theater company again?"

"Knight Players. They were rehearsing a play at the Phoenix." Even though Grant kept his voice level, Patterson could sense his frustration. "You provided them with a hefty sum of money."

"Thirty-five thousand dollars," Patterson added.

"Now I remember. Yes. The theater company's director approached me through my charitable foundation. He was looking for a grant. I told him the foundation was tapped out for the rest of the year. We'd already allocated the money to other endeavors. But I'm a big supporter of the arts, so I made a personal investment instead. Gave the man a loan with a small but fair return."

"And this had slipped your mind?" Grant looked incredulous.

"My foundation gives out a lot of grants, and I make investments in a large number of projects annually. It's hard to remember every individual transaction."

"Still, kind of hard to forget about that much money."

"Are you going somewhere with this, Special Agent Grant, or is it just a fishing expedition?" Russo's lips curled into a thin smile. "I'm well aware that the FBI has been monitoring my activities for more than a decade, even though I'm a legitimate businessman with nothing to hide."

"Sure, you are," Grant said. "And I'm the tooth fairy. We both know your legitimate businesses are just a front for less savory enterprises."

Russo's smile didn't falter. "And we both also know you can't back that accusation up with a shred of evidence. Isn't that right?"

"Tell me about Jeremy Knight," Grant said, ignoring Russo's jab. "Why did you give him so much money?"

Russo shrugged. "Why not?"

"Because legitimate or not, you're a businessman. You want a return on your investment, and the Knight Players were an unproven venture with nothing but an unproduced play to their name."

"What can I say? Jeremy Knight was a persuasive individual." Russo didn't seem phased. "Besides, I love the arts and my community. What better way to give back."

"You're sticking with that story?"

"Why wouldn't I?"

"Because Jeremy Knight is dead. Murdered in a rather gruesome fashion."

"How dreadful," Russo said. "I'll have a bouquet sent to his widow."

"That's mighty kind of you." Grant leaned forward. "But I have to wonder if you had anything to do with Mr. Knight's untimely demise. It must have annoyed you that ticket sales were slow. Practically nonexistent, in fact. Makes it hard for you to recoup your money."

"I won't lie. I expected better, but that's the risk you take as an investor. Some you win, some you lose."

"You don't strike me as the type of person who likes to lose."

"Does anyone?" Russo asked. "Look, I know where this is going. You think I gave Jeremy Knight too much money and then got mad when he couldn't repay it."

"Did you?"

"I didn't kill him if that's what you're asking. His show

might have been a disappointment, but there was still a chance he could turn it around. Maybe people would turn out on the night. Pay on the door. It's hardly in my best interest to kill a man who owes me that much money, which would guarantee I'll never see a penny of it again." Russo paused. "Not that I'm the type of person who would kill a man in the first place, you understand."

"Oh, I understand." Grant looked at Patterson. "You got any questions?"

"Just one," Patterson replied. She turned her attention back to Russo. "How did the two of you meet? I mean, it's clear you didn't move in the same circles."

"I don't remember," Russo said. "Could've been any number of places. Arts benefit. Chamber of Commerce. Hell, maybe I met him in a bar. Stranger things have happened."

Grant stood up. "Thank you for taking the time to talk with us, Mr. Russo."

"You're welcome." Russo walked to the door with the two agents. He held it open for them. "Feel free to come back anytime. When Lighthouse Point opens next month, I can treat you to a meal in the restaurant. We have a Michelin-starred chef lined up."

"Really?" Grant said as they stepped out into the sunlight. "Maybe I *will* come back and see you again."

TWENTY-TWO

AS THEY WALKED BACK to the car, Patterson cast a glance over her shoulder toward the portable building. Bruce Russo stood in the doorway, watching them leave. When he saw her eyes upon him, he gave her a parting wave. She turned her head quickly forward again. "We have a new suspect."

"Looks that way," Grant said.

"He has a point, though," Patterson said as they reached the car. "It makes no sense to kill the man to whom you've just given a pile of money if you ever want to see any of it again."

"Doesn't mean he didn't do it." Grant reached into his pocket as his phone rang. He answered and lifted it to his ear, then hung up after a brief conversation with a look of satisfaction on his face. "The office got a match on that partial plate we sent them. There's only one truck in the state with a license plate bearing those last digits and guess who it belongs to."

"Bruce Russo?" Patterson said, eyeing the assortment of heavy-duty pickup trucks scattered around the construction site.

"Nope. Try our other suspect."

"Stephen Canning?" Patterson's eyes flew wide. "He told us he hadn't seen Jeremy Knight in months."

"He was lying, as people who commit murder often do." Grant was already on the phone again. "I'm calling this in to Suffolk County PD. I'm sure Detective Ahlstrom will be only too eager to swing by Canning's workplace and pick him up for us. I think it's time we get the truth, don't you?"

It was almost five in the evening when Grant and Patterson arrived at the East Hampton Police Department, which was where Ahlstrom had taken Stephen Canning. The detective was waiting for them when they entered and led them wordlessly back to the department's only interview room.

When they entered, Canning looked up. "Decided to go ahead and arrest me after all, huh?"

"You just made it so easy for us," Grant replied, settling into a chair across the desk from his suspect.

Patterson took the second chair next to Grant, while Detective Ahlstrom stood leaning against the closed interrogation room door with his arms folded.

"Am I going to need a lawyer?" Canning asked.

"You've been read your Miranda Rights already, yes?" Grant asked.

Canning nodded.

"Then you already know the answer to that question," Patterson said. "Are you formally requesting a lawyer?"

This time Canning shook his head.

"Can you answer me verbally, please?"

"No."

"You sure about that?" Grant said.

"I haven't done anything wrong." Canning looked down at the table and the handcuffs binding his wrists. "Doesn't matter, anyway. I can't afford one."

"We can have the Public Defender's Office send someone over," Patterson said.

"Those clowns? I had a public defender last time. Didn't do me any good then, won't do me any good now."

"Very well," Grant said. "Since you've made it abundantly clear that you wish to proceed without a lawyer, I'll get right to the point. You lied to us."

Canning hesitated, a look of panic passing fleetingly across his face. "I didn't lie, not—"

"You might want to think about what you say next," Patterson said. "We know you weren't telling the truth about your last contact with Jeremy Knight. We have surveillance footage of your truck parked outside the Phoenix Theater on the night of the murder."

Canning didn't reply. He merely shuffled his feet and continue to look down.

"Nothing to say for yourself?" Grant asked.

"Maybe because he knows he's guilty," Ahlstrom chipped in from behind them.

"I didn't do it." Canning looked up now, anger flashing in his eyes. "This is why I didn't tell you before. Because you'd just assume I killed Jeremy and lock me up."

"Did you kill him?" Patterson asked in a soft voice.

"No. Like I said before. I'm not sorry he's dead, but I didn't do it."

"The evidence suggests otherwise," Grant said. "How about you tell us what happened that night?"

Canning nodded. "I did go to the Phoenix Theater that night, but it wasn't to kill Jeremy. I went there to confront him. Ever since Linda kicked him out, he's been parading his girlfriend around town like he's proud of his cheating. The same college student he got fired and lost his marriage over. The girl is half his age. It was embarrassing. My sister is well-liked. People know her. I was going to tell him to stop, but…"

"Go on," Grant urged. "What happened next?"

"I parked up outside the theater and went down the alley to the stage door. I didn't even know if I'd be able to get in, but it was unlocked. At first, I couldn't find Jeremy, but then I saw him. He was lying in the orchestra pit, and it was obvious he was dead."

"And you didn't call the police to report what you'd found?"

"What do you think? I have a criminal record. I also have a motive. Cops aren't going to look too hard for anyone else after that." Canning's voice trembled. "I panicked and ran back out, jumped in my truck, and got the hell out of there. I figured no one would even know I went to the theater looking for Jeremy that night."

"But we do know," Patterson said. "And right now, your story doesn't sound very convincing."

"I know how it sounds. If only I'd waited one more night to go find Jeremy, I wouldn't be in this mess. But if anyone's the killer, it was probably the other guy."

"What other guy?" Grant exchanged a glance with Patterson.

"The one who was in the alley when I went to the stage door. He was big. One of those men you wouldn't want to meet in a dark alley at night if you'll pardon the pun."

"You get a look at him?"

"Not a good one. All I know is he was wearing a windbreaker and a baseball cap pulled down low. He only looked at me briefly, and his face was in shadow, but I think there was a logo on the cap. Some kind of triangle with three letters inside. I don't remember what they were. He was walking toward Main Street, but then he turned and took off in the opposite direction like he didn't want to walk past me."

"You see where he went after that?"

"Don't know. He turned left at the end of the alley, past the theater, and I didn't see him again. That's when I went in and found Jeremy. Figured Baseball Cap Guy was probably the killer fleeing the scene. That's why he turned tail when he saw me. Guess I got lucky. I mean, what if he decided to off me too rather than leave a witness?"

"That's the story you're sticking with?" Grant asked.

"Yeah. Because it's the truth. Look, if you want to find

Jeremy's killer, you should probably start searching for that guy in the baseball cap."

"The one you can't describe."

"Like I already told you, it was dark."

"One more question," Patterson said. "Jeremy Knight's younger girlfriend. Do you know her name?"

"Sure. Kaylee Robinson. She was in his theater arts class."

"You sure about that?" Grant exchanged a surprised glance with Patterson.

"Hundred percent. She used to work part-time in the coffee shop down the block from the theater. Served me all the time. It's her, alright. I've seen them together myself." Canning looked past Grant and Patterson toward Ahlstrom. "Am I free to go now?"

Ahlstrom pushed away from the wall and stepped closer to the table. "You aren't going anywhere except a holding cell for the foreseeable future."

Patterson looked at Canning. "You might want to reconsider getting that public defender now. I have a feeling you're going to need one."

TWENTY-THREE

"I CAN'T BELIEVE THIS," Patterson said as they made their way out of the building. "Jeremy Knight was dating Kaylee Robinson."

"Looks like Stephen Canning wasn't the only one lying to us." Grant unlocked the car and got in. "I'm beginning to feel a bit like a Yo-Yo. Driving all over town to interview people, only to return when we find out they're not telling the truth."

"I guess we can add Kaylee to the list of suspects now," Patterson said. "After all, she did discover the body."

"Along with another actor," Grant said. "And don't forget, our current lead suspect discovered the body first. At least if you believe his story. He just didn't tell anyone."

"You want to go have another chat with Kaylee?" Patterson pulled her door closed and clicked her seatbelt.

"What do you think?" Grant said as he pulled away from

the curb and started back toward Montauk. "This is getting more convoluted by the minute."

"Jeremy Knight sure created a mess for himself," Patterson said as they left East Hampton behind. "It's kind of sad, really."

"Most murder cases are," Grant replied.

Patterson lapsed into silence and reflected upon this. She watched the landscape speed by beyond the passenger side window and wondered if her sister's disappearance resulted from a similarly convoluted set of circumstances. Patterson hoped not. She always imagined her sister living a new life under some other name, staying away from the family for motives known only to her. It was a nice fantasy, but ultimately Patterson knew it was a lie. There was no reason for Julie to walk away from her loved ones. The truth was a bitter pill and one Patterson didn't want to swallow. In all likelihood, her sister had been murdered.

"Here we are again," Grant said, pulling Patterson out of her maudlin thoughts.

She looked up to find that they were parked outside of Kaylee Robinson's home for the second time in two days.

Kaylee was at the door before they'd gotten halfway up the path. "Did you find out who murdered Jeremy?"

"That's not why we're here," Grant said. "You weren't entirely truthful with us during our last visit, were you, Kaylee?"

"I don't know what you mean."

"I think you do," Patterson said as they drew close.

Kaylee stared at them for a moment, then said, "You'd better come in."

Once they were inside, Grant got right to the point. "You were Jeremy Knight's girlfriend."

Kaylee answered with a rueful nod.

"A fact you neglected to mention the last time we were here," Patterson said. "Would you mind telling us why?"

"I didn't think it was relevant," Kaylee said. "And it was also none of your business. My relationship with Jeremy was private."

"Can't have been that private," Grant said. "Linda Knight's brother saw the two of you out and about. He claimed a lot of other people did, too. Doesn't sound like you are being very discreet."

"Look, I can't help it if Linda and her family didn't like the fact that Jeremy and I were dating. But the truth was, we were in love."

"He lost his job because of your relationship," Patterson said. "Were you aware of that?"

"Of course I was. The college was just being petty. Closed-minded. It was ridiculous. We were both adults."

"Except you were his student, and the college had a strict policy regarding such things."

"That's not my problem." Kaylee motioned toward the sofa. "You want to sit down?"

"No, thank you. We'll stand if it's all the same with you." Grant folded his arms. "This doesn't look good, Kaylee."

"I didn't kill Jeremy if that's what you're implying. I loved him. Besides, I was in the pub along with the rest of the cast when he was murdered."

"We're aware of that," Patterson said.

"And I'm the one who found him."

"We know that, too," Grant said.

"It was awful. I haven't slept a wink since. I don't know what I'm going to do now. We had plans together. He promised to get me work on Broadway. We were moving to New York City."

"He was a teacher," Grant said. "How was he going to do that?"

"He had a stage career before working for the college. He told me that losing his job was a blessing in disguise. That he'd decided to get back into the business. He said I was a natural and that he would take me with him. The play was just the first part of our plan. Once the divorce was final, and he was free of that woman, things were going to be different."

"You believed that?"

"Why wouldn't I?" Kaylee paused, her lip trembling. "I really did care for him. I thought we were going to make it big together."

"Did the rest of the cast know you were dating?" Patterson asked.

Kaylee nodded. "We hadn't made a point of telling them, but people talk. I'm sure they knew."

"Why didn't you stay with Jeremy that night when the rest of the cast left?"

"He often stayed late. Pretty much after every rehearsal, actually. He preferred to work alone when he was rewriting or working on new blocking. He hated distractions."

"Then it would have been common knowledge that he would still be in the theater after rehearsal."

"I suppose." Kaylee shrugged.

"And that he would be alone," Grant said.

"Yes. As I already mentioned, he'd stayed in the theater alone after pretty much all of our rehearsals. He wanted everything to be perfect, and the rewriting was easiest for him when the problems were fresh in his mind."

"I see."

"He always joined us in the pub, though. Eventually."

"Which is why you returned to the theater when he didn't show up?" Patterson asked.

"Yes. He'd been longer than usual, and I was worried." Kaylee sniffed and wiped a tear away. "I still can't believe he's gone."

"It will get easier," Patterson said. "With time."

"I hope so," Kaylee replied. "You have any more questions?"

"No. Not at this time. We'll let you get back to your evening," Grant said, moving toward the door before turning back to the young woman. "Do you have any out-of-town travel planned for the immediate future?"

"No." Kaylee shook her head.

"Good. Make sure it stays that way, at least for now. If I have more questions, I want to know where you are."

TWENTY-FOUR

THEY ATE a late dinner at a French restaurant in town after leaving Kaylee Robinson's house. Patterson was suspicious of the young woman's motives for hiding her relationship with the victim and said as much. But she did, Grant pointed out, have an ironclad alibi. She was in the pub along with the other actors in the play when Jeremy Knight was killed. Regardless of her motivation for lying, Kaylee was not the murderer. That didn't mean he thought she was completely innocent. He just didn't know how she fitted into the puzzle yet.

Later, as they were finishing up a dessert of crème brûlée, sharing the delectable dish because they were both reaching capacity, Grant received an email from Detective Ahlstrom. Attached were Jeremy Knight's cell phone records for the preceding month.

Back at the hotel, Grant forwarded the message to Patterson and asked her to open the attachment on her laptop. They sat around the small table in her room and went through the records for the next hour. Most of the numbers were local, and it didn't take long to discover who they belonged to. Knight had placed calls to his divorce lawyer, soon-to-be ex-wife, girlfriend Kaylee Robinson, and the Phoenix Theater. There were also two incoming calls and one outgoing to Bruce Russo, who was probably checking up on his not-so-stellar investment. But it was the series of calls, both incoming and outgoing, to a number with a Boston area code that caught their eye. There were fourteen, including the last call their victim had received. It lasted for a little over a minute and had a timestamp of 8:17 PM.

Patterson drew in a sharp breath. "This narrows the killer's window of opportunity."

"It does, indeed." Grant studied the phone records with keen interest. "We know that Kaylee Robinson discovered the body around nine o'clock. Still plenty of time for our murderer to slip in and do the deed."

"I wonder who he was talking to," Patterson said, eyeing the multiple calls to and from that number over the previous month.

"Why don't we find out?" Grant said, picking up his phone. He dialed the number and waited. It rang once, twice, three times before the voicemail kicked in. A female voice identified the numbers belonging to Helen and asked them to leave a message.

Grant ended the call without doing so.

He waited a few minutes, then called again with the same lack of success before putting the phone down with a sigh and looking at Patterson. "It appears that we'll have to wait until tomorrow to discover who our victim was talking to in the moments before he died."

"We have a name. That's a start."

"Helen. And judging by the voicemail greeting, the number is personal, not business."

"She might have called back if you'd left a message," Patterson said.

"And she would also know the FBI was calling. If our mystery woman in Boston has some part to play in Jeremy Knight's death, I would rather not give her warning of our interest."

"Makes sense," Patterson said. "I guess there isn't much more we can do tonight."

"Except get some much-needed sleep," Grant said, standing and walking toward the door. "I'll see you in the morning."

"You bringing coffee again?" Patterson flashed her partner a wide grin.

"Doesn't sound like I have much choice," Grant said, stepping out of the room. "Any special requests?"

"How about you bring some pastries this time, too?"

"Don't push your luck."

"Is that a no?"

"We'll see," Grant said, then he turned and pulled the hotel room door closed, leaving Patterson alone for the night.

She turned her attention back to the computer and Jeremy Knight's phone records. Her gaze lingered on that last number-the one with the Boston area code-and she couldn't help but wonder what he'd said on that call, not realizing it would be the last conversation he would ever have. Patterson pondered this for a while, then dragged her eyes away from the screen. She would find no new clues by staring at that list of phone numbers. Not tonight. She closed the laptop and stood, taking her jacket off and unbuckling her shoulder holster with some measure of relief. Placing these on the bed, Patterson went to the mini fridge and took out a two-liter bottle of Coke. She twisted the cap off and was about to pour herself a drink when her eyes drifted to the ice bucket sitting next to the sink.

Coke tasted better with ice.

She hesitated a minute, then made up her mind and grabbed the bucket. Taking her room key, Patterson went to the door and opened it, then stepped out onto the sidewalk and closed the door again behind her.

The hotel was not full. Only half the parking bays were occupied. She glanced toward the room next to hers, where a sliver of light escaped through drawn curtains. Grant would be inside. She heard the low mumble of the TV and wondered what he was watching. A sudden ache of loneliness overcame her, and she almost reached out and knocked on his door to ask if he'd like some company. Not as two FBI agents on the job, but as something more. Friends who enjoyed each other's company. But she didn't. If Grant had wanted Patterson's companionship, he wouldn't have run off the way he did. She thought about Kaylee and Jeremy. Student and teacher. Were the thoughts drifting through her mind any different? She was a rookie agent fresh out of Quantico, and he was a supervisory special agent. Her superior. Better not to even go there.

Patterson lingered a moment longer outside of Grant's room, as if she were hoping deep down that he would appear in his doorway and invite her inside, and then forced herself to keep going in search of the ice machine.

A little further along the breezeway, a set of metal steps led up to the hotel's second floor. Next to them, attached to the wall, was a sign that promised ice and vending further along the block. She picked up the pace, her attention focused on the vending area that she could now see was at the far end of the block, near another set of steps. Which was why she didn't notice the car at first. It was parked several spaces away from Grant's vehicle in a pool of darkness between two lampposts. Ordinarily, Patterson would pay no heed, except that the lights were off, and the engine was running. Inside, she could see faint movement even though she couldn't make out the occupant's features.

A tingle of unease crawled up her spine. She debated returning to the room without ice. But that was ridiculous. So what if a car was idling in a hotel parking lot? It was probably someone checking in. After all, the car was from out of state. A yellow New Jersey plate was affixed to the front.

But then, as she drew closer, the car started to move. It backed out of the space and rolled slowly toward her with the lights still off.

Patterson froze. There was something about the car's movement she didn't like. It was menacing. Now she realized something else. The space it had occupied afforded a perfect view of the rooms occupied by herself and Grant.

The feeling of unease magnified threefold. She reached

instinctively for her gun before remembering it was on the bed back in her room.

A stupid lapse. But then, she was only going for ice.

The car inched forward, drawing closer.

She saw only the silhouetted outline of a head and shoulders through the vehicle's windshield, but somehow she knew the occupant was looking straight at her. At that moment, she forgot all about the ice. Instead, she turned and started back toward her room, resisting the urge to run, while the car with New Jersey plates crept along behind.

TWENTY-FIVE

PATTERSON'S HOTEL room door was only twenty feet away, yet it felt like a mile. She could sense the car rolling along at a snail's pace behind her, even though she dared not take the time to glance around. But she held her breath and listened, waiting for the telltale click of a car door opening and footsteps coming up from behind.

If someone tried to grab her, drag her back toward their vehicle and bundle her inside, she would scream. That should bring Grant running, gun in hand. And any would-be abductor would soon find themselves outmatched. Unless she didn't get the chance to scream. What if they put a hand over her mouth or slipped the muzzle of the gun into the small of her back and told her not to make a sound?

Patterson was not entirely defenseless. Her instructors at Quantico had taught her how to disarm an assailant, but there was a big difference between practicing such maneuvers in the safety of the classroom and doing it in real life, where the gun could go off and send a bullet through you.

She quickened her pace, the door now tantalizingly within reach. And still she heard no sign of the car's occupant exiting his vehicle. She had no doubt that the person stalking her was male because that was the sense she got from the vague outline glimpsed through the windshield. The shoulders were broad, the head large.

After what seemed like an eternity but couldn't be more than thirty seconds, Patterson reached her hotel room. The key card was still in her hand, but in her haste to hold it against the card reader, she almost dropped it. Taking a deep breath, she tried again, and this time she managed to place the card against the reader panel. A gratifying click rewarded her as the lock disengaged.

Patterson yanked on the door handle and pushed, almost tumbling into the room, then closed the door behind her and engaged the deadbolt.

She dropped the empty ice bucket and ran to retrieve her gun from the bed, then raced to the window and cracked the curtain wide enough to afford a view of the parking lot.

It was still and quiet.

The car was nowhere in sight.

She moved to the door and pressed her eye against the peephole, examining the wide-angle view of the sidewalk and closest parking spaces, but saw no one.

She drew the deadbolt back and inched the door open wide enough to step through, keeping the Glock ready at her side. In the movies, people often poked their guns out of the door or around the corner like some kind of advanced guard before they stepped out themselves. That was not a good idea in real life. A would-be assailant could grab the weapon and turn it back on you before you even saw them. But she need not have worried. The sidewalk outside her room was empty. She was alone.

Patterson turned her head, scanning the parking area to see if the driver of the mystery car had found a more discreet parking space further afield, and turned off the engine. He hadn't. There were no vehicles with New Jersey plates.

Patterson pulled her door closed and hurried along the sidewalk towards the registration office, where a cut-through led to the other side of the building. Maybe the car had circled around and was now parked at the motel's rear. But this wasn't the case either. The rooms on the back side were mostly dark. She counted three with faint light escaping the windows past drawn curtains. There were four vehicles in this parking lot, including a newer model quad-cab truck with a fifteen-foot trailer attached parked along the back fence straddling four spaces, but the car with New Jersey plates was not here either.

Her unease subsided a little.

Maybe she had misread the situation, and the vehicle was not watching the rooms occupied by Grant and herself. For all she knew, it was just a weary traveler who pulled off the highway to check out the motel's amenities and then decided against it. But even as she told herself that, Patterson knew better. Someone had been watching them.

She cast one more glance around the parking lot, then hurried back to the front of the building toward her room. She briefly considered knocking on Grant's door and letting him know what had happened, but his window was dark now, and she couldn't hear the TV. He was probably asleep.

Deciding it could wait until morning, Patterson stepped back inside and engaged the deadbolt before getting ready for bed. Normally, she would return the gun to its holster, but not tonight. Instead, she put her gun on the nightstand within easy reach. She also left the bathroom light on, which bathed the room in a comforting half-light. Darkness was not her friend. Then she lay awake, tired but unable to fall asleep, and listened to every unfamiliar sound coming from the motel around her. And all the while, she kept her eyes fixed upon the door just in case the occupant of the car with New Jersey plates decided to return…

TWENTY-SIX

THE NEXT MORNING, Patterson told Grant what had happened when she went to fetch ice. He listened, sitting at the desk in her hotel room, and sipped coffee with a troubled look on his face, but didn't speak until she finished.

"You should have come straight to me last night rather than try to deal with it on your own," Grant said, sounding irritated. "What if something had happened to you?"

"There wasn't time. I already wasted valuable seconds getting my gun. I didn't want the guy in that car to get away."

"He did, anyway. Besides, it would only have taken a second to knock on my door or call me."

"I know. I'm sorry." Patterson realized that going after the car alone had been a mistake. But in the heat of the moment, all she could think of was finding out who was watching them. "When I couldn't find the car, I thought about knocking on your door. But the light was off and I couldn't hear the TV, so I figured you were asleep."

"You should have woken me anyway," Grant said. "If there really was someone watching us, we might have been able to drive around and find them. They couldn't have gotten far."

"I didn't think of that," Patterson admitted. "I won't make the same mistake again. Promise."

"Make sure you don't." Grant set his coffee cup on the table. "Is there anything else you can tell me about the car?"

"No. Not really. It was a sedan with New Jersey plates. Dark-colored. Probably black. Like I said already, it was dark, and I couldn't really see the occupant very well, but I got the sense they were male."

"All of our suspects live in the State of New York. It's unlikely any of them would own a vehicle with New Jersey plates."

"But not impossible," Patterson said. "Or maybe there's a suspect we haven't identified yet."

"Maybe." Grant looked thoughtful. "Is it possible you got spooked and misread the situation? We are in a hotel off the highway, after all."

"I wondered that, too. But I don't think so. There was something menacing about the car. The way it followed me. Hand on heart, I thought someone was going to jump out and attack me from behind, maybe even try to abduct me."

"If what you're saying is true, then we've attracted the killer's attention." Grant stood. "I wonder if the hotel has a security system?"

"If it does, they might have caught the car on camera."

"That's what I'm thinking," Grant said. He was already on his way to the door. He yanked it open and glanced back toward Patterson, who was still in the t-shirt and sleep shorts she had been wearing when Grant showed up earlier than expected with the now habitual cups of coffee in hand. "I'll go find out."

"Want me to come?" Patterson asked.

"No. I can handle this one myself while you get ready."

"Okay." Patterson nodded and watched Grant leave. She dressed quickly, then went to the bathroom and pulled her blond hair into a tight bun. She applied a light coat of mascara and nothing else. Patterson wasn't one of those girls who spent a lot of time on her appearance. After a quick glance in the mirror to make sure she was professional and presentable, she returned to the bedroom, where she checked her gun and strapped her shoulder holster on. A moment later, Grant returned with a resigned look on his face.

"No luck," he said, stepping into the room. "The hotel has a camera in the lobby that covers the registration desk, mostly because they got robbed a few years back. They don't have any cameras on the outside of the building though."

"That's a shame."

"We'll just have to hope our stalker decides to return."

"And when he does, I'll be ready for him," Patterson said.

"Correction. *We'll* be ready for him."

"Right. That's what I meant," Patterson said, seconds before Grant's phone rang.

He answered and lifted it to his ear. After a brief conversation, he hung up and looked at Patterson. "Guess who's back in town?"

"Ben Ford?" Patterson answered, thinking back to the actor who had accompanied Kaylee the night she found Jeremy Knight's corpse in the theater.

"One and the same. He's at his apartment now. Said we can come right over."

"Fantastic." Patterson grabbed her jacket and pulled it on. "Want me to drive?"

"Sure. Why not?" Grant tossed her the keys to his Bureau car. "Let's go."

TWENTY-SEVEN

BEN FORD WAS tall and skinny, easily topping six feet, with a mop of unruly shoulder-length chestnut-colored hair that made him look a little like a surfer dude, except his skin was white as New England snow.

He observed the two FBI agents standing in the living room of his cramped apartment for a few seconds before speaking. "We were all pretty shaken up by Jeremy's death. I mean, this is Montauk, not some bad neighborhood in Detroit. For the life of me, I can't think who would want to murder him."

Grant listened to the young actor and nodded. "When you went to the theater with Kaylee to look for Jeremy, did you see anyone hanging around?"

"No." Ben shook his head. "Not that I was paying much attention until after we found the body. Poor Kaylee. She must be devastated. It wasn't common knowledge among the cast that she was dating Jeremy, but I knew. We've been friends for a long time, and we'd talk whenever she was upset or needed to vent. I guess she feels safe with me. I'm kind of like her sounding board. She was already going through a tough time before this." He paused. "I really should call and see how she is."

"I think Kaylee would appreciate that," Patterson said. "What do you mean about her going through a tough time already before Jeremy Knight died?"

"I'm not sure it's my place to say anything. She told me in confidence."

Grant gave Ben his best cop stare. "I think you can make an exception under the circumstances."

"Well…"

"Unless you'd like to have this conversation in an interview room."

"What?" A look of panic flashed across Ben's face. "There's no need for that. I guess I can tell you since you're FBI."

"Spill it," Grant said, his voice gruff.

Ben hesitated, his gaze shifting between the two agents, then he started to talk. "Just between the three of us, Kaylee and Jeremy's relationship wasn't going so well. She'd taken me aside in the bar after rehearsal the night before Jeremy died, and she was upset. She wanted my advice."

"Why was that?" Patterson asked. Her own soft tone was a deliberate counterpoint to Grant's abruptness. "You can tell us. It isn't a betrayal of your confidence. I'm sure she wants Jeremy's killer found just as much as you."

"I know." Ben ran a hand through his hair. "She thought

Jeremy was going to leave her after the show. They were going to break up."

"Why would she think that?"

"Because of what she found on his phone. He was taking a shower, and a text message came through. She didn't mean to look, but she saw it pop up on the screen. It was from a realtor in Boston confirming the lease on an apartment there. When he came out of the shower, she pretended she hadn't seen it. Jeremy read the text, then deleted it."

"That doesn't mean he was going to leave her behind," Patterson said. "Maybe he just hadn't told her yet."

"No." Ben shook his head. "There was more. She'd overheard him talking to someone when he thought she was sleeping a few days before. He was planning to open the show in Boston after our run finished. That's why he needed an apartment there. He told the person on the other end of the line that it was a new start for him. Thing is, he hadn't mentioned this to anyone in his cast, so he wasn't taking any of us with him. Including Kaylee. Or so she thought."

"Did she speak to him about it?"

"I don't think so. He was still acting as if nothing was wrong, saying he loved her. He even said they should look for a place together in New York City, which was ridiculous considering he'd already rented an apartment in another town and hadn't bothered to tell her. I think she was afraid and didn't know what to do. She adored him."

Grant and Patterson exchanged glances. First, Kaylee Robinson had failed to mention her relationship with the victim, and now they discovered that Jeremy Knight was planning to leave her once the play was over.

Grant pondered this for a moment, then looked at them. "Was Kaylee in the bar the whole time between the end of rehearsal and when she asked you to accompany her back to the theater?"

"Yes. I'm sure she didn't leave." Ben furrowed his brow. "Look, if you're suggesting Kaylee was the killer, you're way off base. I saw Jeremy in that orchestra pit. Saw what was done to him. I haven't been able to sleep since. It was brutal. Even if Kaylee could have snuck out—and I don't believe she did—there's no way she would have possessed the strength to do something like that. She weighs like a hundred pounds."

"We understand," Patterson said.

"Just to be clear, you're saying that Kaylee was with you the entire time until you discovered Jeremy Knight's body."

"She was in the pub, yes." Ben paused, narrowing his eyes. "The only time she wasn't with the group was when she went to buy drinks at the bar. But that wasn't enough time to leave and kill anyone. Besides, I saw her there talking to some older guy. He was probably hitting on her. It happens."

"You're sure about that?" Grant asked. "She was with you the whole time."

"I guess," Ben said.

Grant said nothing for a moment. Then he looked at Patterson. "I think we're done here."

TWENTY-EIGHT

ON THE CURB outside Ben's apartment, Grant took his phone out. "We need to find out exactly what Jeremy Knight was up to."

"You're calling the Boston number again?" Patterson asked.

"Maybe we'll get lucky this time." Grant was already dialing.

It rang three times, and then a female voice picked up. "Hello?"

"Who is this?" Grant asked, putting the phone on speaker so Patterson could hear too.

"Who's asking?" The voice on the other end replied.

"My name is Jonathan Grant. I'm an FBI agent out of the New York Field Office."

"Umm, that's odd. Have you got any proof?" The woman didn't sound convinced. "For all I know, you're a scammer saying you're with the FBI to steal my identity."

"I can give you my badge number. If you'd like to phone the New York Field Office, they will vouch for my credibility."

"Let's assume you are with the FBI. Why are you calling me? I've done nothing wrong."

"We're looking for information regarding a man named Jeremy Knight."

"Is Jeremy in trouble?" The woman sounded alarmed.

"I'll explain in due course, but it really would be helpful if I knew your name."

"Oh, right. It's Helen. Helen Lang."

"Thank you, Miss Lang," Grant said. "Tell me, what's your relationship with Mr. Knight?"

"You promised to let me know what's going on."

"And I will," Grant said. "But first, I need you to answer some questions. To begin with, how do you know Jeremy Knight?"

"We've been friends for years," Helen said. "We went to college together. We were in the same drama classes."

"Have you heard from him recently?" Grant asked.

"Actually, yes. We lost touch for the longest time, but we reconnected after he separated from his wife. Isn't social media a great thing?"

"Depends on your point of view," Grant said. "When was the last time you spoke to Mr. Knight?"

"I don't know, a few evenings ago. He's going through a nasty divorce and recently lost his job. It's been hard on him, and I've been doing what I can to help him out. It really is awful. The things that woman put him through. He's better off out of it."

"What was your relationship with Jeremy?" Grant asked. "Back in the day?"

"If you're asking what I think you're asking," Helen said, "we were an item throughout college. He was a charmer back then. Still is, actually."

"And now?"

"Things have been getting serious between us. But we're taking it slow. We're both recently out of failed relationships and want to get it right this time."

Grant looked at Patterson. "You're currently dating Jeremy Knight?"

"I suppose you could call it that. We haven't spent much time together yet. At least not in person, given the distance between us. I've driven down to New York, and he came up to see me once. But that will change when he moves here next month. We have everything arranged. We even found him a great apartment in Arlington."

"That's not a cheap neighborhood," Grant said. "You know where he was getting the money to pay for it?"

"Jeremy told me Linda had released some funds from their joint bank account so he could get set up in Boston."

"Really." Grant raised an eyebrow. "Just out of interest, what do you do for a living, Miss Lang?"

"I'm artistic director of The Severn Troupe. It's a small nonprofit theater company with three stages in a converted warehouse building that reopened as an arts center. We're not that well known yet, but we're working on it. We performed at the Fringe this year and received great reviews. With Jeremy's talent, we're only going to get better."

"You offered him a job?" Patterson asked, stepping close

to the phone, then added, "Sorry, I should've introduced myself. I'm Special Agent Patterson Blake."

"I see. Yes, he's coming to work for us. It isn't a full-time gig, but he'll get to put his play on. And in the meantime, he'll be working as a director for our second stage productions."

"Second stage?" Patterson asked. "What's that?"

"They're our smaller shows," Helen said. "Like I said, we have three stages at our facility. The main stage shows are big budget. Musicals and such. Then we do smaller stuff on the other two stages, one of which is a black box. Honestly, Jeremy becoming available is a godsend. It's hard to find good directors."

"When are you expecting him there?" Grant asked.

"A couple of weeks. He'll be leaving pretty much straight away after he finishes the show in Montauk."

"Speaking of which," Patterson said. "Are you acquainted with the cast of his current show?"

"I haven't met any of them, but he told me they're a talented bunch."

"Do you know a young woman by the name of Kaylee Robinson?"

"I don't know her, but I recognize the name. She's the female lead in his show."

"Has Jeremy ever spoken to you about her?"

"He might have mentioned her in passing, but I don't recall any particular conversations. Why do you ask?"

"No reason," Patterson said. "Just tying up loose ends."

"What loose ends?" Helen sounded nervous. "What is all this about? Is Jeremy in trouble?"

"If you're not sitting down, Miss Lang, I think you should do so," Grant said. "I'm afraid we have bad news."

"Has there been an accident?" Helen Lang's voice lifted a half octave. "Dear God, is he okay?"

"No, he's not." Grant paused a moment as if picking his words. "I'm sorry to tell you this, but he died the night before last."

"What?" Helen Lang practically screeched the word. "That's impossible. I talked to him two nights ago after rehearsal. He was fine. Are you sure you haven't made a mistake?"

"Quite sure," Grant said.

"Oh." There was a tremble in Helen Lang's voice. Patterson sensed she was weeping. "He was supposed to call me back yesterday, but I figured he got tied up with the divorce proceedings. His wife was doing everything she could to cause trouble. To be honest, I was surprised she gave him money to relocate. Please tell me, how did he die? Was it an accident?"

"No," Grant replied solemnly. "It wasn't an accident. He was murdered."

TWENTY-NINE

GRANT SLIPPED the phone back into his pocket. "Well, that was an interesting call. It confirms what Ben told us. Jeremy Knight was planning to leave town."

"And Kaylee was correct in assuming she wasn't accompanying him despite the promises he'd made to her," Patterson said.

"Not if he had another woman waiting for him in Boston."

"You think Kaylee knew about Helen Lang? That would be a good enough motive for murder."

"Beats me." Grant shrugged. "He wasn't being honest with either woman. We know he didn't get the money to rent that apartment from his soon-to-be ex-wife."

"You think he dipped into the cash Bruce Russo gave him?"

"I think it's likely. He had no other sources of income independent of Linda."

"That puts Russo squarely back in the crosshairs. What if he found out Jeremy Knight was embezzling money from his own theater company?"

"Without bank records, we won't be able to confirm where he got the money for that apartment," Grant said. "I can start the process to get them, but it might take a while."

"It seems like everyone had a motive to kill Jeremy Knight," Patterson said. "He doesn't sound like a very nice guy."

"Didn't deserve to be murdered, though," Grant said, walking toward the car. "I think we should pay a visit to the bar where Kaylee and her actor friends went after rehearsal on the night of the murder. I'd like independent verification that she was there the whole time before they discovered the body. Then we can focus our efforts on the other suspects."

"It's still early. They might not be open yet," Patterson said, looking at her watch.

"Let's go over there and find out," Grant said, climbing into the car. "Kaylee neglected to tell us she was in a relationship with the deceased until we confronted her. Then she forgot to mention his plans to leave town without her. Acted like everything was rosy between them. I'd like to know what else she isn't being truthful about."

They were in luck. McGee's Irish Bar was open when they arrived. A sandwich board out on the sidewalk advertised a full Irish breakfast available from 8 AM onwards. Patterson's gaze lingered there for a moment. Their own breakfast had comprised nothing but coffee. When they left the bar, she would suggest a stop at Dunkin' before they went anywhere else. But first, they had to confirm Kaylee Robinson's alibi. She stepped past the sandwich board and followed Grant inside.

McGee's was dimly lit and decked out in dark wood wainscoting below forest green walls. Patterson had been in plenty of Irish pubs over the years. New York was full of them, and this place could pass for any of a hundred dotted across the city. Mirrors advertising beer products from Bass to Guinness hung between an assortment of old-world items like washboards, musical instruments, rowing boat oars, and sepia-toned photographs that cluttered every vertical surface in a mad jumble. There were few patrons at this time of day. A group of men that looked like they might be in construction sat around a table eating near the back. A young couple relaxed near the window, sipping coffee and watching the world go by.

Grant approached the bar with Patterson a step behind.

The bartender was a slim woman who Patterson guessed to be in her early forties. She had dark hair pulled back into a ponytail and wore an apron. At their approach, she looked up with a smile.

"What can I get for you?" She asked.

"How about some information?" Grant replied, flashing his credentials and introducing them both.

"If it's about that nasty business down at The Phoenix, I've already spoken to the police." She dropped a rag she'd been wiping across the bar. "The name's Jodie, by the way. I'm the owner of this fine establishment."

"You don't sound very Irish," Grant said.

"I'm not. But my husband is. County Kerry. He's not here right now."

"Hello, Jodie," Patterson said.

Jodie nodded a greeting and folded her arms. "About the other night, I can't tell you anything I haven't already told the detective who came in here."

"I understand. We have your previous statement," Grant replied. Despite his unfriendly demeanor, Ahlstrom was keeping them in the loop. "But I would like to confirm some details for myself."

"Tell you what, you make it worth my while by having a nice Irish breakfast, and I'll answer all the questions you care to throw at me."

"You trying to coerce federal law enforcement officers?" Grant asked, a smile playing on his lips.

"No, sir. I'm trying to keep my business afloat, which isn't easy when cops keep coming in asking about the violent murder a block down the street."

"Fair enough. We'll take two breakfasts." Grant looked at Patterson. "Hungry?"

"I was thinking of picking up a doughnut after we left here," Patterson replied. "But I guess a plate of greasy fried food will do just as well."

"That's the spirit." Grant turned back to Jodie. "I'll take my eggs over easy."

"Done." Jodie scribbled out an order and took it back to the kitchen. Returning, she leaned on the bar. "Now, what do you want to know?"

"Do you recall seeing the cast of Jeremy Knight's show in here two evenings ago?" Grant asked.

"Sure. They came in just like they always do after rehearsal. They're a friendly lot."

"You know them well?" Patterson asked.

"Not by name or anything, but I know their faces."

"We're interested in one cast member in particular," Grant said. "A young woman by the name of Kaylee Robinson. She was playing the lead. Twenties. Long blonde hair. About five feet four with a slight build. Sound familiar?"

"She was here," Jodie replied. "Bought a round of drinks. Nice enough girl. Gave me a decent tip."

"You remember if she left here at any point?"

"This is a bar, hon. People come and go all the time. I don't pay attention."

"Then you can't confirm how long she was here?" Patterson asked.

"As I said, people are in and out all the time."

"That's no help to us," Grant said, disappointed. "We still only have the word of her friends that she was here, and for all we know, they're covering for her."

"You could try the security footage," Jodie said, pointing up to a camera mounted above a shelf at the end of the bar, its single black eye staring out into the room. "I offered to let the other cops see it, but they weren't interested."

"You have a recording of the evening in question?" Grant asked.

"Sure. We record continuously. That way, if a fight breaks out or something, we've got it all on tape for later. Not that we have much trouble in here, mind you." She added quickly. "We're a family-friendly establishment."

"Can we see the tape?" Patterson asked, her hopes rising.

"My pleasure. I already pulled that evening's footage and saved it just in case the cops changed their mind and came back." Jodie motioned for them to follow her through a door marked private at the end of the bar. As she passed by the kitchen, she pushed the door open and shouted inside. "Hey, Marty, cover the bar a minute, will you? I'm taking these people into the back office."

"Sure," a gruff voice responded from somewhere beyond the door.

"Thanks." Jodie let the door close and led Grant and Patterson into the office, which looked more like a cramped stockroom than anything else.

Cages full of liquor lined two walls, the doors held closed with heavy padlocks. There were beer barrels and crates of soda stacked high. Patterson and Grant stepped around them and saw a small desk with an old computer tower attached to a monitor. Jodie settled in front of the desk and pulled up the footage, fast-forwarding to the moment when the troupe of actors entered the bar. And there she was. Kaylee Robinson. Laughing and chatting mutely with her friends on the silent video footage. At least until she approached the bar and started a different conversation with a gentleman who stood with his back to the camera. A thickset man wearing a windbreaker and a baseball cap.

THIRTY

"THAT'S HIM," Patterson said excitedly. "The man that Linda Knight's brother claimed he saw in the alleyway near the stage door on the night of the murder. It has to be. He's wearing a windbreaker and baseball cap."

"Or it could be a random person hitting on Kaylee," Grant said. "Just like Ben thought it was."

"Come on, you don't believe that. It's too much of a coincidence."

"It doesn't matter what I believe," Grant said, his eyes still focused on the video footage. "We can't make a murder case based on nothing more than the back of a man's head."

"This sucks," Patterson said. She leaned over Jodie's shoulder and peered at the screen just as the figure in the baseball cap turned to pick up a drink.

And there it was. His face was still in shadow, but the triangle logo was clearly visible on the baseball cap. And inside the logo were three initials. RPD.

Patterson drew in a sharp breath and glanced at Grant. "Will that do it for you?"

"It's getting there," Grant said. "But we still don't know who he is."

"Well, he's wearing a cap with a logo on it. That's a good place to start looking."

"You're right," Grant said, taking his phone out and tapping away on it. A moment later, he turned the screen so that she could see it. "Look familiar?"

"I don't believe this," Patterson said, staring at the website displayed on Grant's phone. Russo Property Development. And in the banner at the top of the site, the triangle logo with the initials RPD inside, just like on the cap. "Why would someone from Bruce Russo's company be talking to Kaylee?"

"Your guess is as good as mine." Grant's attention was back on the computer monitor now. "Coincidence seems like a bit of a stretch given what we now know."

"Can we do anything to make the video brighter?" Patterson asked, looking down at Jodie. "It's so grainy."

"Sorry. It's not exactly well-lit out there. What you see is what you get. Maybe if you sent it to your fancy FBI lab, they could do something, but I just run a bar."

"Do you recognize the person she's talking with?" Grant asked.

"Hon, we get a hundred people a night in this place and more on weekends. Unless they're solid regulars or leave me a five-hundred buck tip, all the faces look alike."

"How about a staff member? Was there someone else working that night?"

"My husband was in the kitchen helping out, and Kelly was working a shift. She's one of the bartenders, but I doubt she'd know any better than me."

"I think we need to talk to her anyway," Grant said.

"I can call her," Jodie replied. "She goes to the local community college during the day, so I can't guarantee she'll pick up. Might be in class."

"If you wouldn't mind trying, anyway."

"Wait. That won't be necessary." Patterson placed a hand on Grant's arm. She was staring at the computer monitor. She addressed Jodie. "Can you rewind the footage and go back just a little way?"

"Sure thing," Jodie said. "Tell me when to stop."

"What are you looking for?" Grant asked.

"You'll see." Patterson crouched down beside Jodie to get a closer look at the screen. After a moment, she cried out. "Stop it there and pause."

"Well, I'll be damned," Grant said. In the video, a man that must have been Jodie's husband came out of the kitchen carrying plates of food. In that instant, just as the kitchen door opened and then swung closed again, bright fluorescent light spilled out and momentarily illuminated the face underneath the cap. "That's Bruce Russo himself."

"Without a shadow of a doubt," Patterson said, feeling pleased with herself.

"How did you even spot that? It was so quick."

"I just happened to have my eyes on the kitchen door at the right time," Patterson replied. "It was over in a flat second, too quick to see anything when the video was playing, but I figured if we backed up and paused it, we might get lucky."

"This doesn't make sense." Grant narrowed his eyes. "What possible connection could there be between Kaylee Robinson and Bruce Russo?"

"Let's find out." Now it's Patterson's turn to bring her phone out. She stood and paced back and forth in the cramped room, browsing the web for several minutes. Then she let out a squeal. "I have it, and this is a doozy."

"Let me see." Grant turned toward her.

Patterson held her phone at arms-length and turned the screen to show him a photograph from several months before on Kaylee's Facebook profile. It showed the young actress standing next to Bruce Russo. His arm was around her shoulder, and they were both smiling. "Look at the caption."

Grant squinted and took the phone from her hand. "*Me and Uncle Bruce.* You've got to be kidding."

"I know, right?" Patterson said, beaming with pride at her discovery. "Kaylee's mother must be Bruce Russo's sister. How did we miss that?"

"Because we weren't looking." Grant handed the phone back to her. "Now it makes sense. Kaylee started dating Jeremy Knight and took the lead in his play. She convinced her uncle to invest in the theater company, thinking it was her ticket to the big time…"

"But then Jeremy embezzled the money to start a new life with another woman in Boston," Patterson said, continuing their deduction.

Grant took up the reins again. "When Kaylee found out

what was going on, she realized Jeremy had used her to get Bruce's investment. He didn't love her."

"I doubt she loved him either," Patterson said. "They were using each other."

"Doesn't matter. Kaylee was angry. Humiliated. She must've told her uncle what had happened."

"And he met her here that night to make sure Jeremy Knight was alone in the theater before he went around there and murdered him."

"And then Linda Knight's brother showed up to have it out with Jeremy, only to find a corpse and flee because he didn't want to be blamed."

"Do you think Kaylee knew her uncle was going to kill Jeremy?" Patterson asked.

"Does it matter? Either way, she's an accomplice to murder at this point." Grant was already dialing Detective Ahlstrom's number. "I'm going to have Kaylee brought in."

Patterson could only hear one side of the conversation. She waited impatiently until he hung up, then said, "Well? What's going on?"

"Local PD is going to find Kaylee and arrest her."

"And Russo?"

"That's down to us. Ahlstrom is sending detectives to the construction site, but it will take them a while to arrive. I don't want Kaylee tipping her uncle off when the cops show up on her doorstep. We'll go over there right now and hold him until they arrive."

"Sounds like a plan," Patterson said, even as she was moving toward the door.

"Wait," Jodie said, following the agents out of the office. "What about your breakfasts?"

"Oh. Right. Forgot about that deal." Grant stopped at the bar and took his wallet out. He placed two twenties on the counter. "That should cover it."

"You don't want to stop and eat?" Jodie sounded disappointed.

"We'll take a rain check," Patterson said, hurrying toward the front door. She felt a tingle of excitement. Soon, there would be one less murderer on the streets. This was why she'd joined the FBI. "We have a killer to catch."

THIRTY-ONE

PATTERSON SAW it the minute they stepped out of the bar. A dark sedan with distinctive yellow New Jersey license plates sitting half a block away. She nudged Grant and drew his attention to the vehicle. "That's the car I saw last night in the parking lot."

"And now it's here," Grant said. "I guess you were right. Someone *was* surveilling us."

"And I want to find out who," Patterson said, starting toward the car at a clip.

"Slow down." Grant caught up with her and grabbed her arm. "Don't make it obvious or you'll spook them." But even as he spoke the words, the car edged out of its parking space and rolled down the street toward them.

"Too late." Patterson stepped between two parked cars and into the street as the sedan drew level with them, reaching for her gun at the same time. The car swerved around her and kept going, then picked up speed.

"Come on," Grant said, sprinting toward their own car. "Get in."

Patterson slid the Glock back into its holster and ran to the passenger door. "I got their plate number," she said, making a note on her phone so she wouldn't forget.

"Good to know." Grant swung onto the road and pressed the accelerator down hard to catch up with the sedan. But it had already turned off Main Street and by the time they reached the side road, the other car was nowhere in sight.

"They can't have gotten far," Patterson said, looking around.

"If all else fails, I'll call the plate in and get an address, but I'd rather not wait that long. Did you get a look at the driver?"

"I caught a glimpse as he drove past. It wasn't Bruce Russo."

"I wouldn't expect it to be," Grant said. "He has plenty of employees he could send to watch us. People involved in his less than legal endeavors."

"Which means they might be on their way back to warn him at this very moment. That guy could easily have slipped into the bar and overheard us talking."

"Then we're about to lose the element of surprise." Grant was already heading toward Lighthouse Point, Bruce Russo's hotel construction site. Now he sped up. "I hope they trained you well at Quantico, Special Agent Blake, because our investigation might just have taken a dangerous turn."

"I can handle myself," Patterson said. And it was true. She had qualified with high marks in both her firearms training and hand-to-hand combat. But even as she spoke the words, Patterson felt a twinge of apprehension. What if she wasn't ready? But there was no time for self-doubt. She could see the rising tower of Lighthouse Point's namesake building as they drove along the road, skirting the shore of Montauk Lake. And then they were upon the construction site and turning in.

"That's the car we're looking for," Grant said, bringing their own vehicle to a stop behind the now familiar dark sedan, which was parked near a pair of pickup trucks about fifty feet from the newly erected hotel buildings. "I don't see any sign of the driver."

"That's because he's probably inside already," Patterson said. "Which means Bruce Russo will be expecting us."

"Can't do anything about that." Grant opened the driver's door and stepped out, reaching for his service weapon at the same time.

He waited for Patterson to join him, and together they set off toward the hotel.

When they reached the sedan, Grant placed a hand on the hood. "Still warm. Definitely the right car."

Patterson nodded and glanced around, a tingle of foreboding weaving up her spine. The last time they were here, it was abuzz with activity. Now it was silent, and she could see no workers anywhere. "I don't like this. It doesn't feel right."

"Maybe everyone's inside," Grant said, although he didn't sound convinced.

"Maybe." Patterson slipped a hand inside her jacket and

took her gun out. She glanced up at the hotel's dark windows, wondering if they were being observed.

A moment later, she had an answer.

A sharp crack echoed across the construction site. Patterson recognized the sound right away. A rifle.

She reacted instinctively, diving sideways to put the sedan between herself and the shooter. She expected Grant to do the same, but when she looked around, he wasn't by her side anymore. And then she saw him lying motionless on the ground, his shirt stained crimson with blood.

THIRTY-TWO

GRANT!" Patterson screamed, hoping he would answer. Praying he wasn't dead. The senior field agent lay on the ground six feet from the car, which meant he was probably within the gunman's field of view. She had to pull him out of the line of fire before a second bullet found her partner. Taking a deep breath, she risked a peek up over the car's hood to locate the sniper.

No sooner had she revealed herself than a second shot rang out. The slug buried itself in the vehicle's hood inches from her head with a dull smack. She ducked back down, her heart thudding against her rib cage, but she had gotten the information she needed. When he fired, the shooter had revealed himself to be on the second floor of the hotel. The muzzle flash was a giveaway.

Patterson steeled herself and gripped her gun tight. She took a deep breath to steady her nerves, then pivoted, lifting herself up just enough to get a clean shot at the open window without making herself an easy target. She fired two rounds in quick succession, then ducked back down and scrambled toward Grant's prone form, hoping her return fire would momentarily distract the gunman.

She slipped her hands under his armpits and heaved, dragging him back toward the car and safety.

He groaned and opened his eyes, looking up at her. "Did I get shot?"

"Just a little bit," Patterson replied, feeling a rush of relief at the sound of his voice. But then her gaze fell to his blood-soaked shirt, and the dread crept back. It looked bad. Really bad. But at least he was alive.

Grant pulled himself up against the side of the car and sat there breathing heavily. He probed his chest gingerly with two fingers and winced. "Feels like more than a bit. I think the bullet got me in the shoulder. Can't tell if it went clean through."

"There's so much blood," Patterson said. "We have to get help before you bleed out."

"Not until that gunman's taken care of. I heard you return fire. Did you get them?"

"Maybe," Patterson said, then changed her mind. "I don't think so."

"There won't be any help on the way then. Not unless we want to get someone else shot."

"Which is why I have to take care of this." Patterson was aware that valuable seconds were ticking away. She reached into Grant's pocket and removed his phone, then dialed 911. She put it on speaker and held the phone toward Grant. "Call it in."

"What are you going to do?" Grant asked, pressing one hand against the wound to staunch the flow of blood and taking Patterson's phone with the other.

"Secure the area. Take care of any active shooters."

"Patterson—"

"Don't tell me it's not a good idea. If I don't do this, you will die."

"I was going to say be careful," Grant replied just as the 911 dispatcher came on the line, asking about the nature of the emergency. He looked at Patterson and mouthed one word. *Go.* Then he turned his attention to the phone.

Patterson didn't need any urging. She moved to the front of the car, keeping low. She gauged the distance to the pair of parked pickup trucks. It wasn't very far, but far enough to get her shot if she wasn't careful. No one had fired on their position in at least thirty seconds, but that didn't mean their assailant had given up. He might be biding his time, knowing that Grant was down, and waiting for her to break cover. But there was nothing she could do about that. Expecting to become a target the second she came into view, Patterson hunkered low and launched herself toward the trucks as fast as her legs would carry her.

The distance between the sedan and the two pickups couldn't have been more than fifteen feet, but to Patterson, it felt like an eternity. Yet miraculously, she made it with no more shots ringing out and was soon sliding to a halt behind the first truck.

Either the shooter couldn't get a bead on her, or he'd realized firing on federal agents was a bad idea and fled. It made her feel a little better about the next open space she would have to traverse in order to reach the hotel building. And this one was a longer distance. At least forty feet. Plenty of opportunity to catch a bullet.

She glanced back toward Grant, propped up against the sedan. He wasn't talking to the 911 dispatcher anymore. He sat slumped with his left hand on the floor, the phone still held in it. Patterson was pleased to see his other hand remained pressed against the wound, but blood was seeping through his fingers. He didn't look good. An icy dread enveloped her. Grant might die, after all. This was what everyone in law enforcement dreaded. Losing their partner to a senseless act of violence. It was made all the worse because this was her first proper field assignment, and she liked Grant.

No. It was more than that. There was an attraction she hadn't felt for a man in years, mostly because of her single-minded devotion to becoming an FBI agent. She had let her personal life take a hit. Now, just when she could ease up a little, the one man she felt something for—even though she didn't know if the feeling was mutual—might not live long enough for her to say anything.

She couldn't let that happen.

Until the scene was cleared of active shooters, Grant wouldn't be able to receive medical attention. His life was in her hands. With a new sense of determination, Patterson sized up the gulf of open space between the truck she was currently sheltering behind and the open doors to the hotel lobby.

She tensed her muscles, dug her feet into the sandy soil, and pushed off with her gun held high. But instead of making a beeline for the doors, she veered to the right, then to the left, in a zigzagging evasive pattern, just like the tactical instructor at the academy said to do.

And a good thing too.

A slug smashed into the ground inches from her foot, sending up a plume of dirt.

The gunman hadn't given up. He was just waiting for her to present a better target.

Patterson raised her own gun toward the window where she'd seen the muzzle flash minutes earlier and squeezed off two rounds in rapid succession.

A trio of shots raked the ground in answer, too quick for individual trigger pulls. She swore under her breath. Whoever was up in that window must have an assault rifle, probably an AK-47, and it was now in burst mode.

She returned fire, suddenly aware that if she reached the hotel and came face to face with the shooter, she would be outgunned.

But that didn't matter. Grant was depending on her.

Besides, she was close to the building now. Another few feet and the gunman wouldn't be able to fire down upon her. His angle would be too steep. That was something, at least.

But no sooner had the thought run through her mind than she heard another rat-a-tat of gunfire. And this time, the shooter had anticipated her position.

She cried out as white-hot pain lanced through her body, and then Patterson was tumbling forward onto the hard-packed earth. And in that moment, she wondered if this was what it felt like to die.

THIRTY-THREE

PATTERSON LANDED on the ground hard enough to expel the air in her lungs with a mighty whoosh. Her rib cage burned with pain under her left arm, and it hurt when she drew breath.

She crawled forward toward the building, hoping it would take her out of the sniper's field of view, then reached around and probed the area with her fingers, terrified she had been shot in the chest and was now on borrowed time. Instead, she found torn fabric and what appeared to be a flesh wound under her armpit. It had been close. A couple of inches to the left and she would be dead. But miraculously, the bullet had only nicked her.

Realizing she might still be in the gunman's crosshairs, Patterson heaved herself up and stumbled forward toward the hotel doors. She barged through, letting them slam back behind her, and scanned the half-completed lobby.

It was empty, and no one had fired upon her when she stepped inside, which meant the shooter must still be on the second floor.

Patterson hurried to the grand staircase that led up to what appeared to be a mezzanine level. She took the steps two at a time, ignoring the stab of pain that flared in her chest every time she sucked air in. When she reached the first floor, Patterson paused again, her gaze sweeping the wide-open central concourse. The floor was still bare concrete. Large rolls of carpeting in plastic wrap were stacked waiting to be installed. Tools were strewn around. A gantry stood toward the back, under a section of ceiling with air conditioning ducts exposed. What she assumed to be conference rooms led off on each side, their doors closed.

She saw a bank of elevators to her right blocked by barricades with signs warning they were not yet in use.

Further away, she spied a door marked stairs and headed toward it, her senses on high alert in case the shooter appeared. If that happened, she would have only a moment to react.

But no one appeared. She reached the door without incident and pushed it open as quietly as she could. The stairwell beyond was dimly lit by temporary work lights spaced at intervals up the stairs.

She raised her gun and peered upward.

All clear. At least so far.

The person who shot Grant and almost killed her must still be one level up. Unless they had made their escape through another stairwell, which was certainly possible. They were sure to know the building better than Patterson.

Either way, she had to make sure.

Patterson started up the stairs, her footfalls dull on the concrete steps. She reached the half landing and pivoted, aiming her gun up toward the second-floor doorway above, but no one lay in wait for her.

Patterson sprinted up the remaining steps. She cracked the door open and peered into the corridor beyond. The construction was almost complete on this level. Dark red carpet covered the floor below pale gold painted walls. But the lighting fixtures were still missing, their location marked by bare wires hanging down. Instead, more work lights illuminated the corridor, casting pools of brightness amid the gloom.

She eased the door open and stepped into the corridor, turning to the left after making a mental calculation that the muzzle flash had come from a room in that direction, although it was impossible to know which one.

She went to the closest hotel room that overlooked the construction site and tried the door. It opened into a partly furnished space with a bathroom on one side. The carpet underfoot smelled fresh. There was a desk and two nightstands. A mattress still wrapped in plastic stood against the wall in front of the door. Patterson eased past it, satisfied the room was empty, and went to the window. She could see Grant's car below still parked behind the New Jersey sedan. She couldn't see Grant, but assumed he was still sheltering behind the vehicle. Or he had bled out and was already dead.

That thought made her gut tighten, and she pushed it away. She told herself he was going to be all right. All she needed to do was find the shooter and eliminate him, then help could reach her partner.

Stepping away from the window, Patterson hurried through the room and returned to the corridor beyond. She moved on to the next door. This room was empty, too. She entered the corridor a second time and turned right. She was about to check the third hotel room when she heard a shuffling, dragging noise.

Patterson spun around in time to see a burly figure appear further along the corridor. She recognized him as the driver of the dark sedan. And in his hands, the AK-47.

"Don't move," Patterson barked, bringing her own weapon up. "Armed federal agent. Drop the gun. Now!"

But the man didn't discard the rifle. He lifted it higher, bringing the muzzle to bear on the FBI agent.

"Don't do it." Patterson's finger tensed on the trigger of her Glock.

But then the man slumped sideways, his shoulder hitting the wall. His head dipped forward toward his chest, then jerked up again, as if he were struggling to remain conscious. The AK's barrel slid down until it was pointing more toward the floor than Patterson.

He pushed himself away from the wall and took a faltering step forward under one of the temporary work lights, and Patterson saw the reason for his sluggish advance.

He'd taken a bullet to the gut. A slow and painful way to die. She must have gotten lucky with one of her blind shots toward the location of the muzzle flash. But now, as the lifeblood seeped out of him, the sniper was fading fast. She doubted he had enough strength left to lift the heavy assault rifle to his shoulder let alone shoot, but she kept her finger on the Glock's trigger, just in case.

"Put the gun down and I'll get you medical help," Patterson said, more to diffuse the situation than because she believed he could be saved.

The gunman looked at her with watery eyes that were clouding over even as she spoke. The AK's muzzle swung lower still toward the ground. He took another unbalanced step, then his legs gave way, and he dropped to his knees, the assault rifle slipping from his grasp and clattering harmlessly onto the floor. He fell sideways against the wall before pitching forward and ending up face down on the newly installed carpet, which was already turning a darker red underneath him. Patterson hurried forward and used her foot to push the AK-47 out of the man's reach. She kneeled next to him and checked for other weapons before placing two fingers against his neck to confirm what she already suspected. The sniper was dead.

But Bruce Russo was still very much at large.

No sooner had this thought entered her head, than she felt a silent vibration in her pocket. She slipped her gun back into its holster and pulled her phone out.

Grant's name appeared on the screen.

Thank God. He was still alive.

She hit answer. "Grant?"

"Not quite," a voice said on the other end of the line. "Your partner isn't doing so well."

Patterson's stomach churned. She recognized the man who was calling on Grant's phone. It was the person they'd come here to arrest.

Bruce Russo.

THIRTY-FOUR

"WHERE'S GRANT?" Patterson asked, her objectivity giving way to blind rage. "What have you done with him?"

"I haven't done anything with him… yet." Russo let out a dry chuckle. "I assume you're still in the hotel looking for my colleague?"

"I found your hired goon already." Patterson knew she shouldn't goad the man who clearly held Grant's life in his hands, but she couldn't help herself. "He isn't looking too hot, either. In fact, I think his days of shooting people are over."

"Shame. I imagine killing a man will create a lot of paperwork for you." Russo sounded out of breath. "If you want to stop your partner from joining him in the great beyond, I suggest you stay put until I'm out of here."

"You must know that isn't going to happen." Patterson was already racing for the stairs. "You're not getting away.

Neither is your niece. The police will have picked her up by now."

"And my lawyers will get any charges dropped. You have no proof she did anything wrong."

"We have her on surveillance video meeting you in McGee's right before the murder," Patterson said, flying down the stairs at a breakneck pace toward the mezzanine. "At the very least, she'll be an accessory. Not only that, but she'll talk. Spill everything about your involvement."

"Maybe. But it won't matter. All your proof is circumstantial, and I have a lot of money. By the time you find me, I'll already have bought enough judges and district attorneys to make this go away." There was a pause on the other end of the line. "Goodbye, Special Agent Blake."

"Wait," Patterson screamed, but Russo had already hung up. She cursed under her breath and ran across the mezzanine, then down the grand staircase to the lobby.

When she got outside, Patterson skidded to a halt, looking around frantically. There was no sign of Bruce Russo. But she did see something else that made her heart soar.

Jonathan Grant.

He was right where she'd left him, propped up against the sedan with New Jersey plates. Even better, he was still alive.

When he saw her, he raised an arm, gesturing feebly.

She dashed across the construction site, veering around the trucks that had provided cover from the sniper earlier, and dropped next to him.

"Russo," he said through clenched teeth. "He was here. He took my phone and gun. I was too weak to stop him."

"It's okay," Patterson said, dismayed to see how much blood Grant had lost. She wondered where their backup was... the paramedics... Detective Ahlstrom and his men. Then she realized it hadn't been that long since the first shots rang out. They were probably still on the way. "Don't talk. Save your energy."

"He went that way," Grant said, trying to raise his arm and point. "Toward the marina."

"I'll take care of it." Patterson took her gun out again and rose. "There's no way I'm letting that man escape."

"Be careful," Grant said, his voice ragged. "I don't want to lose you."

"You won't." Patterson looked down at Grant, her eyes meeting his. "Promise me you won't die while I'm gone."

"I'll try." Grant coughed and grunted in pain. "Go get the bastard."

Patterson didn't need any urging. She gripped her service weapon tightly, and ran back toward the hotel, relieved that this time, no one was taking potshots at her from on high. The wound under her armpit where the sniper's bullet had grazed her burned with each step, but she ignored it and kept going. It was nothing compared to Grant's injuries.

When she reached the building, Patterson paused. The marina was on the other side of the hotel. She could either go around the outside, which would waste valuable minutes, or through the lobby toward the expansive glass wall overlooking the lake and hope the doors there were unlocked.

It was a gamble.

If she chose the wrong option, Russo would escape after all.

Patterson was momentarily frozen by indecision, then she threw caution to the wind and decided the shorter route through the lobby would be preferable. And she took off again, pushing through the hotel's wide front doors. Her footfalls rang on the marble floor as she hurried toward the back of the building, skirting the grand staircase and extravagant statue Russo had been installing last time they were here. She gave no thought to the gunman on the second floor. He was no longer a threat thanks to a well-placed bullet from her Glock, and she was pretty sure the building was otherwise empty.

She could see the marina now through the wall of glass that made up one entire side of the lobby. It stretched along the lake's bank from the hotel all the way to the faux lighthouse, which sat near the water. Piers pushed out into Lake Montauk, with boat slips on both sides. These would be home to expensive yachts and cabin cruisers once the hotel opened. Right now, they were empty. She wondered why Russo had fled in this direction. And then she saw it. A lone bowrider moored in one of the last slips, sleek hull glistening in the sunlight as water lapped against it. She saw something else, too. A figure near the lighthouse, running toward the boat. And it could only be one person.

She found the doors leading out to the marina and

tugged, aware that if Russo reached the boat, she would lose him.

The doors didn't open.

Locked. She'd made the wrong decision, after all.

She considered running back through the lobby and taking the long way around, even though she knew it would take too long. Then an idea occurred to her. Patterson stepped back, removing her Glock from its holster at the same time.

She raised the gun and aimed at one of the glass doors, then squeezed the trigger.

The Glock's report mixed with the sound of the bullet's impact into the door made Patterson wince.

The glass held together for a split-second, turning suddenly opaque. A thousand cracks raced across its surface. A moment later, it shattered onto the floor in a hail of small granular pieces.

Patterson rushed forward, crunching over the broken beads of glass. She sprinted across an open deck overlooking the water, then descended onto a gravel pathway skirting the marina.

Russo was making his way along the furthest pier and was almost at the boat.

If he'd heard the gunshot, he wasn't paying it any heed.

Patterson raced after him. By the time she reached the pier, he was about to step into the bowrider.

"Stop right there," she screamed, advancing toward him, and bringing her Glock to bear.

"I had hoped my little ruse with your partner would buy

me more time." Russo turned to face her. "I figured if you thought he was in danger you might hold back."

"That isn't what I do," Patterson responded. She closed the gap between them. "Move away from the boat, I'm bringing you in."

Russo observed her with a steely gaze. "I don't think so." He took a step toward the bowrider.

"I said stop." Patterson's finger tensed on the trigger.

"Why?" Russo turned back toward her. "You won't shoot me. I'm unarmed. That would be murder."

"You didn't care about that when you bludgeoned Jeremy Knight to death with a hammer." Patterson knew Russo was lying about being unarmed. He'd taken Grant's service weapon. It must be hidden somewhere about his person. She would have to be careful.

"I didn't intend that to happen," Russo said. "I went there to confront the man. Put the fear of God in him. He was stealing my money to disappear and start a new life. I wouldn't have seen a penny of it back."

"You killed him over a few thousand dollars?" Patterson asked, unable to help herself.

"No. I killed him because he messed with my niece. She's family and we look after our own. When I heard that lowlife scum on the phone in the theater talking to another woman, I knew he was irredeemable."

"And you decided he didn't deserve to live."

Russo shrugged. "There was a toolbox with a hammer in it. Some stagehand must've left it when they were building the set. Seemed like too good an opportunity to pass up. You know, he actually begged for his life at the end. It was pathetic."

"I think I've heard enough," Patterson said, reaching for her handcuffs. "Keep your hands where I can see them and lay face down on the ground."

"Sure," Russo said. But he didn't keep his hands where she could see them. Instead, he made a lightning-fast motion behind his back, and before Patterson realized what was happening, she was staring down the muzzle of Grant's gun as Russo brought it up and pulled the trigger.

THIRTY-FIVE

PATTERSON HAD ANTICIPATED that Russo would do something like this. She launched herself sideways out of the line of fire and squeezed off three rounds of her own even as bullets from Grant's stolen gun whizzed through the air mere inches from her head.

A pair of her own bullets sailed harmlessly past the desperate mobster.

The third found its mark, driving him backward with a pained grunt.

She landed hard on the deck and rolled, stopping herself at the edge of the pier, inches shy of ending up in the water. The jolt coaxed fresh waves of pain from the wound under her arm, but she couldn't think about that right now.

There were still plenty of bullets in Grant's gun, and she didn't know how badly injured Russo was. Making an assumption that he was out of action might be a fatal mistake.

Patterson scrabbled to her feet and turned, ready to shoot again, but the property developer and mobster turned killer was no longer a threat.

He was standing at the end of the dock with a surprised expression on his face. The gun had slipped from his hand and now lay harmlessly on the wooden boards of the pier. His polo shirt, a bright canary yellow, was slowly turning red. He looked at Patterson and opened his mouth as if he wanted to say something, but all that came out was a strange croaking sound. Russo stood there a moment longer, swaying once, then he toppled sideways and disappeared from view with a splash between the pier and the boat.

Patterson felt the tension drain from her body, even as she heard a wail of approaching sirens carried on the breeze.

Backup had finally arrived.

She walked to the edge of the pier and looked down into the murky water. Bruce Russo was nowhere to be seen. Deciding it was someone else's problem, Patterson bent over and picked up Grant's service weapon. She slipped it into her shoulder holster and kept her own gun at the ready, just in case there were any more surprises. After casting a quick glance around, she started wearily back toward the mostly finished hotel building and her injured partner waiting beyond.

THIRTY-SIX

THE NEXT DAY

PATTERSON SAT in a chair next to Grant's hospital bed with a book open on her lap. It was almost noon, and she had been at the hospital for more than four hours already. She had tried reading but found herself distracted and now sat lost in thought as he slept to the steady beep of an electrocardiogram machine.

After the shootings at Bruce Russo's construction site, she had been put on administrative leave by Marilyn Kahn, the Special Agent in Charge of the Criminal Investigative Division at the FBI's New York Field Office. This was standard procedure, and she hoped to be back at the Bureau within days. But for now, Patterson was free to spend time at her partner's bedside.

"Hey, you," Grant said in a weak voice.

"Hey." Patterson looked up, surprised to find Grant

awake and looking at her. He'd almost died from blood loss at the construction site and then flatlined twice in the back of the ambulance.

"How long have you been here?"

"A while," Patterson said. She had let the paramedics patch her up on site and then taken the Bureau car to the hospital, driving like a crazy person behind a police cruiser escort detective Ahlstrom had arranged. Later that evening, when they took him into surgery to remove the bullet that was lodged in his chest dangerously close to his heart, she paced back and forth in the waiting room, praying he wouldn't die. Marilyn Kahn had been there too, her stony demeanor temporarily replaced by one of concern for the wounded agent. When the doctor came out to let them know the surgery was over, and Grant was stable, Kahn had finally convinced Patterson to leave and get some much-needed sleep. But unwilling to leave her partner's side for long, Patterson had returned to the hospital at first light. "I was so worried about you."

"Me too," Grant said, forcing a smile that ended up looking more like a grimace. "I thought I was a goner, for sure."

"You almost were," Patterson replied. "It was touch and go there for a while."

"What about you?" Grant asked. "You didn't look too hot yourself the last time I saw you. You were bleeding."

"It's nothing. A bullet grazed my ribs. That's all."

"Sounds like you are lucky."

"We both were."

"And Bruce Russo?" Grant tried to sit higher in the bed

to see her but grunted in pain and gave up. "Please tell me he didn't get away."

"He didn't." An image of Russo standing at the edge of the pier with bright scarlet blood staining his shirt flashed through her mind. He looked surprised that she'd shot him, even though he was trying to kill her. "He won't be causing any more trouble."

"He's in custody?"

"He's dead. At least so far as we know," Patterson said. "He went into the water after I shot him. Suffolk County PD and the USERT dive team have been searching the lake since yesterday evening but haven't found the body so far."

"If he's there, they'll pull him out," Grant said. USERT was the acronym for the FBI's Underwater Search and Evidence Response Team. The divers were highly trained and good at their job.

"I hope so."

"You're sure he's dead?"

"Sure as I can be." Patterson nodded. "Even if the bullet he took to the chest didn't do the job, he wouldn't last long in that water."

"And Kaylee Robinson?"

"Sitting in a jail cell." Local police had arrested Kaylee at her house the previous afternoon and were holding her as an accessory to murder. And with no one to pay them, Russo's high-powered attorneys hadn't leaped to her defense. Unless someone else in her family had money, it looked like she would end up with a public defender. "She's in a heap of trouble."

"All of her own making," Grant said.

"The detective interviewed her already. She's not talking. Claimed she knew nothing about her uncle's intentions toward Knight. The meeting in the bar was purely social, and she didn't realize he was going to the theater afterward."

"She'd hardly say anything else," Grant said.

"Except that her friend Amber cracked under questioning. Said that Kaylee was angry and wanted Knight to pay for betraying her. Told the interviewing officer that on the morning of the murder, Kaylee admitted she had a plan to get even with him. Said that by the end of the day, Knight would be sorry he ever lied to her."

"A woman scorned," Grant observed.

"Precisely."

"Still doesn't prove premeditation," Grant noted. "But it does blow a hole in Kaylee's claim of innocence. She plotted with her uncle to harm Jeremy Knight, and even if the original intent was just to scare or rough him up, the result was Knight's death at Russo's hand. That's still second-degree murder."

"Which is why she's looking at an aiding and abetting charge. She's facing years in prison."

"What about Knight's brother-in-law, Stephen Canning?"

"Ahlstrom let him go," Patterson said. "He might be rough around the edges, but he didn't commit a crime."

"At least, not this time." Grant turned his head to meet Patterson's gaze. "How does it feel to crack your first case?"

"Not so good," Patterson admitted. "Not when my partner is lying in a hospital bed because of it."

"If it weren't for you, I'd probably be lying a few floors down in the morgue."

"Don't say things like that," Patterson replied. "You're here, and that's all that matters."

Grant watched her for a moment, then reached out and took her hand. "And you're here beside me, which makes it even better."

"I'm glad you think that." Patterson squeezed his hand and looked into Grant's eyes. "Because I'm not going anywhere."

"Good." Grant settled back into the pillows and closed his eyes with a contented sigh. "Now go back to reading your book. All this talking has made me tired."

SISTER WHERE ARE YOU SNEAK PEAK

Read on for a sneak peak of the Patterson Blake Series Book 1.

Available Now

PROLOGUE

SIXTEEN YEARS AGO

SHE SURFACED to a sensation of motion and a world of darkness. At first her thoughts were disjointed, as if she were coming around from a night of heavy drinking. Her throat was dry too, and it hurt when she swallowed. But she hadn't touched any alcohol. This was different. She had been drugged. It was probably the glass of iced tea she'd drank to stave off the terrible thirst that had become her constant companion.

She was dressed now, but not in her own clothes. Those were long gone. The garments she currently wore felt baggy on her size six frame—at least three sizes too big. She couldn't remember getting dressed, which meant he put them on her after she passed out. That she wore no underwear was further proof she had not dressed herself.

"Where are we?" she asked in a croaky voice, as the realization dawned that she was being carried over her captor's shoulder like a sack with her arms pulled behind her back, wrists tightly bound. "What's going on?"

Silence was her only answer. He rarely responded to her questions, no matter how many times she asked. He had spoken little during her months of captivity, and when he did, it was to issue terse commands like *take your clothes off*, *stop crying*, or *look into my eyes*. He said that last one the most, forcing her to gaze at him while he abused her. Now, though, something had changed. Instead of leading her from the block building to his cabin, nestled among densely packed elm and cedar trees, he had knocked her out.

This frightened her more than anything. She knew there had been others before because she'd found a name scratched into a floorboard under the metal frame bed with the stained mattress.

Helen.

She'd tried to add her own name but hadn't succeeded. There was nothing inside the room with which to make a mark except her fingernails, and all she'd managed to do was break two of them. Afterward, she'd cried for a long time, not because of the pain, but because writing her name alongside that of a previous captive made her feel less alone, even though she suspected Helen was long since dead. Now she wondered if her predecessor had awoken one night, groggy and afraid, being carried half-naked through the woods, just as she currently was.

"I'm uncomfortable," she said, trying again. "Can you please let me walk?"

"We're almost there," her captor responded, hitching her

further over his shoulder and gripping the back of her leg with a powerful hand.

"Almost where?" She tried not to let the fear show in her voice. From somewhere behind them, she could hear the distant sound of lapping water. Was there a stream nearby? A lake?

"You'll see."

She lapsed into silence, realizing the futility of her questions. Besides, the answer might be worse than not knowing. She suppressed a sob, swallowing hard to contain her terror. The filthy outbuilding he'd kept her in for so long didn't seem so bad now she was faced with the unknown. She almost begged to go back there but knew it wouldn't work, just like all the begging that preceded it hadn't.

Not that it mattered. He was slowing up now, coming to a halt. He pitched her forward off his shoulder and let her slide to the ground. Leaves crunched underfoot as she struggled to maintain balance. Then he shoved her forward toward a black shape looming up out of the earth.

She realized it was an old automobile with sweeping lines and chrome hubcaps surrounded by whitewall tires, the air inside them long since escaped. Leaves and other decaying matter covered the hood and roof in a thick vegetative carpet. The car was reminiscent of the one her grandfather kept in a garage at the back of his house and only drove when he was going to auto shows, except his vehicle didn't have vines growing up over the wheel arches and dirt caking the windshield.

He steered her toward the derelict vehicle and tugged at the rear door, pulling it open on protesting hinges.

An odor wafted out, pungent and ripe.

Ignoring the smell, her captor lifted a foot and put it behind her knee, applying enough pressure that she buckled, even as he placed a steering hand atop her head and pushed her forward with the other. She felt herself pitching into the car, and found the will to fight back, digging her heels into the soft earth next to the vehicle. She twisted and bucked, overcome with a sudden sense of her own mortality. But her captor was too strong, and she was soon bundled inside, hands still restrained behind her back. The stench was worse now. Like rotting cabbage tinged with garlic. She gagged and tried to hold her breath.

A flashlight clicked on, bathing the car's interior with a dull yellow glow. Then she saw the chain, one end draped over the front seat. The other disappeared underneath.

The man reached in and took the chain. He looped the free end around her neck a couple of times, tight enough that she gasped for air. A padlock appeared from his pocket, which he inserted between the loops and clicked shut. He tugged on the chain to make sure it was secure, then stepped back, dangling an item between two fingers for her to see. A pair of small silver padlock keys. He dropped them into the leafy detritus on the hood too far for her to reach. Then he leaned in close, his mouth inches from her ear, and spoke in a soft voice. "I'll never stop thinking about you."

With those parting words, he slammed the car door and stepped back. He watched for a moment as if admiring his handiwork. Then he turned and retreated through the forest, the beam from his flashlight getting fainter until she was left alone.

Except she wasn't totally alone.

As the moon emerged from behind scudding clouds, a ray of silvery light spilled through the back window, illuminating the chained corpse sitting next to her in the back seat. In the front was a second body reduced to little more than skeletal remains with patches of dark, mottled skin attached. She knew it was female only by its clothes. A rotten sweatshirt and a stained yellow skirt. The corpse sat bent slightly forward, giving the grimy windshield a dead stare, one bony hand shackled to the steering wheel with a set of rusty handcuffs.

She screamed and flinched away from her long-dead companions, tugging at her restraints in a desperate attempt to escape. But it was no use. The chain was too tight, and there was no one around to hear. Except for the man who had brought her here, assuming he was still within earshot. Which was why she cried out for his help, even though she knew it was useless.

Her captor did hear the girl's terrified pleas. He turned off the flashlight and stood in the darkness, soaking up her terror as she shrieked and begged for him to return. Then, after the screams had given way to exhausted whimpers, he continued down the overgrown woodland trail with a satisfied smile on his face. And as he went, he wondered how long it would take her to die.

FAMILY STATEMENT
IN THE DISAPPEARANCE OF JULIE BLAKE — SEPTEMBER 20, 2005

On September 20 of this year, our 19-year-old daughter, Julie Blake, was reported missing to the Los Angeles Police Department after she did not return home from a summer cross-country trip. All attempts to contact her have failed.

Julie is a wonderful and vivacious person. Her love for adventure and passion for life have inspired her family and friends in so many ways. We do not believe she would voluntarily break off contact.

If anyone knows where Julie is, or they have information regarding what happened to her, we urge them to contact the LAPD or their local police. Callers may remain anonymous if they so desire.

Julie, if you are out there and see this, please call. We are worried and want to know that you are safe, regardless of whether you wish to return home. We love you, always.

— Mom, Dad, and Sis.

POLICE STATEMENT
IN THE DISAPPEARANCE OF JULIE BLAKE
— NOVEMBER 14, 2005

The Los Angeles Police Department has concluded its missing persons search for Julie Blake, a 19YO student attending college in Chicago, Illinois. Julie was reported missing by her family after she failed to return from a summer road trip, however we have uncovered no evidence that she disappeared under suspicious circumstances. We are no longer actively looking for Julie. We would like to thank all those involved in the investigation. Out of respect for the family, we will make no further statements at this time.

ONE

NOW

FBI SPECIAL AGENT Patterson Blake weaved her way through the mess of rusting farm machinery clogging the barn she had entered moments before. She moved forward on high alert, gripping her Glock 19M service weapon with both hands, trigger finger pressed to the frame. Although it was pointed downward, Patterson was ready to bring the gun up at a moment's notice, but she hoped it wouldn't be necessary.

From somewhere outside the barn, in the direction of the dilapidated farmhouse, she heard shouts—other agents identifying themselves prior to entering the structure. More agents would be fanning out across the property, fifteen of them in total, all with the same objective. To locate the man who lived here and any victims that might still be alive.

Patterson slowed her step, searching the gloom between

the pieces of equipment. To her left was a tractor, the back wheels almost as tall as she was. Next to this was a plow attachment with three large blades. Further away she could make out what looked like a tiller. The other side of the barn was crammed with oil drums, an old truck with the hood missing, and a riding mower. It was clear that none of it had moved in years.

She reached the middle of the aging structure. Ahead of her another set of double doors just like the ones she'd entered stood open, spilling an oblong patch of sunlight across the barn floor. She took one more look around before moving faster again, deciding she was alone. But as she neared the exit, a faint noise somewhere behind the tractor drew her attention.

Patterson swiveled, raising the gun.

The sound came again. A faint scrabbling that sent the hairs on the back of her neck standing on end.

She aimed toward the movement and spoke with all the authority she could muster. "Armed federal agent. Keep your hands where I can see them and show yourself."

Her command went unheeded.

Patterson stood listening to the stirring air within the barn, waiting for something to happen. When it didn't, she repeated her warning and edged forward, stepping between the tractor and a multi-bladed attachment that looked as much like an ancient torture device as it did a piece of farm equipment. But when she reached the other side of the tractor, nothing was there.

She felt her thumping heart ease up, just a little. She turned to make her way back toward the barn doors, lowering the gun once more, just as the sound came again. This time though, she caught movement from the corner of her eye. Bringing the service weapon back up, Patterson curled a finger around the trigger ready to fire. But she didn't need to. Instead of the suspect, she saw a furry gray body hightail it in the opposite direction, ringed tail scraping the ground.

A big fat raccoon.

Patterson felt a rush of relief, but at the same time, she'd had enough of the barn. She circled back around the tractor and hurried to the doors, stepping out into the bright June sunshine. To her right was the farmhouse, a two-story shingle-clad structure with a wraparound porch. It had once been painted white but was now weathered to a silvery gray with only the barest hint of paint remaining. One of the porch's corner posts had rotted causing the roof above to sag. She saw a figure standing near the front door, wearing a baseball cap above a blue nylon raid jacket with the letters FBI written across the back in blocky gold lettering.

Behind the house, across what had once been an open farmyard ringed by a decaying picket fence, stood a second barn, smaller than the one she just searched. It was to this that she now set off, determined to complete her sweep of the outbuildings. She was three quarters of the way across the open area when something caught her eye near the fence line. An oblong spot of disturbed earth that looked darker than the soil surrounding it. It was barely noticeable. In fact, she would have walked right past had the sun not been slanting down at the right angle to cast a shadow across the unusual depression.

Patterson changed course and approached the anomaly. Now that she was closer, it looked less like a depression in the ground and more like something buried. She holstered her gun and kneeled down, then brushed the loose soil away to reveal a sheet of pockmarked and eroded metal. It extended way beyond the area she'd first noticed. A pair of hinges were attached at the far end. Closer, near her knees, a piece of rope was tied through a roughly hewn hole.

This was no sheet of metal. It was a trap door.

Patterson stood and brushed herself off, then gripped the rope and pulled. The makeshift trapdoor swung upward to reveal a dark space beneath. Fetid air belched out. She heaved the door all the way up, then let it fall open with a thud. Pulling a flashlight from her pocket, she dropped to her knees again and leaned over the gaping chasm, turning the light on at the same time.

She aimed the beam down through the hole and was shocked to find an oblong room with corrugated metal walls. With a jolt, she realized it was a shipping container, buried deep in the earth and covered over again to conceal it. Several inches of stagnant water sat on the container's floor. A noxious odor of decay wafted up.

Patterson leaned in further, sweeping her flashlight beam around the concealed space until it picked out a small figure huddled in one corner. A thin young woman wearing a stained and torn blouse, and not much else. She sat with her knees drawn up to her chest, arms folded around her breasts, and head bent low. She wasn't moving, but the barely perceptible whimpering sounds escaping her lips proved the woman was alive. Then, as if sensing the FBI agent's eyes upon her, the girl lifted her head and looked up.

Patterson felt a stab of icy shock. She almost dropped her flashlight. She squinted into the darkness, studying the features of the young woman that gazed back at her, stunned and confused. It was impossible, she knew, yet she could not deny her own eyes. She recognized this girl. A wave of dizziness overcame her, and she reached out, gripping the edges of the trapdoor to stop herself tumbling forward. The world compressed down until there was nothing left but herself and the woman in the shipping container. She gasped for breath, too stunned to move. Until she heard pounding footsteps approaching from her rear. She glanced up to see a middle-aged man, shirtless and obese, lumbering toward her with a pitchfork gripped in his meaty hands. A sheen of sweat covered his doughy skin. His eyes glinted with anger.

Patterson fell backwards and raised her arms in defense, even as the pitchfork arched down toward her chest. The man behind it snarled in anger. She flinched away from the sharp tines, expecting to be impaled at any moment.

Instead, two sharp cracks rang out. The burly man tottered a moment, looking surprised, then fell forward. The pitchfork clattered harmlessly to the ground next to her.

Patterson lay still for a moment, recovering her senses. The girl's face swam in front of her eyes. The face of a person she hadn't seen in sixteen years. She blinked to clear the illusion then glanced up to see Lance Driscoll, one of the senior agents at the New York Field Office, standing several feet away with his gun extended. He approached the man he'd shot, kicking the pitchfork away before kneeling and checking for a pulse. He shook his head. "Dead."

But Patterson wasn't listening. She rolled over and scrambled back to the dark opening in the ground, completely oblivious to the agents descending upon the scene from all directions. She reached into the shipping container, extending a hand toward the figure that still sat huddled in the corner. And as the tears started flowing, she uttered a name over and over again. A name she hadn't said aloud in a very long time. Julie.

Sister Where Are You is available now in e-book, print, and audio

Made in the USA
Middletown, DE
25 October 2022

13501521R00125